Linda Strachan

www.stridentpublishing.co.uk

Published by
Strident Publishing Ltd
22 Strathwhillan Drive
The Orchard
Hairmyres
East Kilbride
G75 8GT

Tel: +44 (0)1355 220588
info@stridentpublishing.co.uk
www.stridentpublishing.co.uk

Published by Strident Publishing Limited, 2012

Cover art by The Earlybird | Cover design by LawrenceMann.co.uk

A catalogue record for this book is available from the British Library.

ISBN 978-1-905537-36-5

Typeset in DIN by oscarkills | Printed by Bell & Bain

The publisher acknowledges support from Creative Scotland towards the publication of this title.

Linda Strachan is the author of over 60 books for all ages. Her first novel for teenagers was the highly acclaimed SPIDER, winner of the Catalyst Teenage Book Award 2010. This was followed by DEAD BOY TALKING, an edgy novel about life, death and knife crime.

Before becoming a full time writer Linda had a variety of jobs, she was a model, a medical lab technician and a fashion buyer. She enjoys doing the research for her novels because it takes her to interesting places and she gets to meet some fascinating people. She likes dogs, painting pictures on walls, artichokes, olives and chocolate, but prefers writing to almost anything else.

For Alexa, Erin, Harriet, Tara and Ciara.
A book needs readers and you are the best, and the first!

Writing is a solitary occupation, but during the process chances sometimes arise to get out and about in the name of research. I like to make the most of such opportunities. As this is a work of fiction, no-one mentioned here bears any responsibility for the way I have used any information gathered in my research. Nonetheless, I would particularly like to thank the following: Stephen Gourlay and David Lockhart of Lothian and Borders Fire and Rescue Service, for taking time to talk to me about fires and arson (firesetting); and Angus Black, for pointing me in the right direction. Many thanks to the lovely Anne Sturgeon, Fiona Melville and the Longniddry Library Teen reading group — Ciara Harvey, Alexa McCraw, Harriet Owens, Erin Ketchion and Tara Cusack for their excellent and thoughtful comments and suggestions.

Thanks to Keith Charters and all at Strident Publishing for their continued belief in me, to Susan Pierce Sloan for her excellent cover design, and special thanks to Alison Stroak, the most encouraging and perceptive editor a writer could ask for.

As ever I am indebted to my family, who are always in my corner, especially my husband, Stuart, for his encouraging support when I am writing and his endless patience and thoughtfulness.

'We often think we are seeing the whole story but sometimes it is like looking through a keyhole, we only see part of the story and that can be bad, real bad, because if we don't see the whole picture the bit we see might be the wrong bit.

It works for people, too. You think you know me, but think again because you don't, so Don't Judge Me!'

FIRE – it yearns to be free, it warms, glows, smoulders, sears and consumes – hot, burning, destructive and terrifying, but above all unpredictable and deadly.

The letterbox was narrow but that wasn't a problem. Peering through it, the light in the hallway showed a patterned carpet, a rectangle of paper on the floor, and the silence of an empty flat.

With a quick twist the bottle cap came off, followed by eye-watering fumes. A bundle of rags, hungry and dry, soaked up the liquid. Gasping at the sharp pungent smell of the accelerator, the saturated rags were pushed through the small oblong opening, to fall beside the paper on the floor.

Fumbling fingers made it a struggle to light the matches. One, two, three all fizzled out; flickers of light in the quiet dark of the night.

Finally, a match flared into life with a shocking, dazzling brilliance and with a cry, waving burnt fingers in the air, it was dropped onto the floor. It flashed, consuming droplets of fuel that dripped from the rag and hissing it died, letting darkness reign once more.

With a rasp a flame tore through the dark, revealing a face in an eager, horrific caricature. Stuffed through the letterbox it touched the metal framing the gap and faded to nothing.

"Again, again!" the grating voice slurred in the onset of panic.

A pure bright light lit up the hallway and burned strongly as it fell flickering onto the rag below. It lay for seconds, the edges of the oblong of paper curling in the sudden heat. With a flash of light the fumes ignited and moved like a contagious illness, breeding tiny flames as it grew. A cloud of black choking smoke rose up inside the door frame, caressing and darkening the paint as it reached higher and higher.

By the time tiny tendrils of smoke curled and danced through the letterbox the figure had turned to run — footsteps beating a staccato on the pavement, disappearing out into the night.

*****

A chilling cry split the air like the shards of broken glass that burst from the window, shattering on the concrete. The choking, grey-black smoke was a dark monster, a billowing volcanic cloud, bubbling up and growing within itself, filling the space around it, consuming the cool, clean, clear air, hiding flashes of crimson as searing flames licked the smoke-darkened stone.

CHAPTER 1

The baby fell through the air.

It plummeted towards the ground.

Suzie looked up, her stomach churning, terrified to take her eyes off it for a second. Its mother was screaming as she watched it fall, screaming at the figures below.

"Save my baby. Somebody, please, save my baby!"

The flames and choking smoke hid her from view as they forced her inside and consumed the building around her.

Suzie stared in disbelief, her pulse racing, eyes glued to the tiny pale shape silhouetted against the black plume of smoke that rose into the night sky.

The baby was falling,

dropping through the air,

dropping...

down...

down...

It was dressed in pink, just like her baby sister.

Leila had been fragile, precious, so soft and warm. Suzie would hold her as Leila looked up with bright eyes and a sweet smile. She would lay her gently in her cot and watch so that no harm would come to her.

Suzie was waiting for someone to do something, to step forward and catch the baby. She couldn't do it, she couldn't. She would drop it, miss it. It would slip through her fingers, landing horribly on the concrete path.

The baby fell,

dropping...

down...

down...

Seconds passed in slow motion...and still the baby fell.

"I can't." Suzie's cry was more of a cracked gasp. An eternity passed as she waited for someone else to run forward.

She couldn't do it. She couldn't move.

She'd had a bit too much to drink, she felt sick and shaky. Someone else would do it, someone had to... they had to...

All around her the crowd was breathless in silence, shocked and scared.

Sirens wailed, impossibly far in the distance. The Fire Service had been called but they were too far away and the small, fragile baby was falling, faster and faster now, falling towards the ground.

Panic surged with hot needles through her veins, her eyes glued to the tiny shape. Why was no one going to help?

The seconds stretched impossibly long, the world had stopped. There were no sounds, nothing else seemed to exist, there was just her and the baby,

dropping through the air,

falling...

falling...

falling...

She couldn't breathe.

In a moment it would be too late but her body was rigid, immobile. She was waiting for that other responsible person, that someone else who would take a step forward just in time. But no one was moving.

From the corner of her eye she could see people around her watching, like marble figurines, surprise and horror mingled in their sculpted faces.

Suzie looked up; it was almost too late.

She ran forward.

Her hands shook as she held them out. The voice in her head said she couldn't do it, but she had to. It was Leila, all over again. In her head there was no difference. The baby was falling,

faster now...

faster and faster...

closer...

closer...

What if it slipped through her hands?

No! Suzie knew she had to save her.

A soft thud.

She clutched the precious bundle tightly, tears streaming down her face, unnoticed. "Hush, hush Leila. I'll keep you safe," she whispered. "See, I caught you. I didn't drop you. You're safe now."

CHAPTER 2

The girl's social worker was running late, which did nothing to sooth DI Larkin's irritation, but they couldn't start until the woman arrived.

He opened the door and beckoned to the WPC waiting outside the room. "Any sign of her yet?"

"She should be here any moment, Sir. She called to say she'd been stuck in traffic, you know what the High Street's like this time of day, but she's just parking her car, now."

The social worker arrived, walking in briskly, smartly dressed and hardly bothering to acknowledge DI Larkin as she swept past him into the interview room. Larkin watched from the door for a moment as she settled herself into the seat next to the girl.

"'bout time!" the girl muttered under her breath, just loud enough for everyone to hear.

The social worker gave a pained look in Larkin's direction but he pretended he hadn't seen it. She opened up her briefcase to take out a pad and pen, laying them neatly side by side.

"Good morning Suzie, this is DI Larkin, but I expect you know that already." Her voice sounded as if it was strained with the effort of being pleasant. "Right, let's get started shall we," she said brightly, as if she'd not been the one who'd kept them all drumming their heels for the last half hour.

Larkin watched the girl for a moment or two as she played with the bracelets on her arm. Her nails were short, bitten to the quick and covered in bright nail varnish that was peeling off. He had no idea what was going on in her head under that spiky mass of dyed blonde hair.

Her foster mother had dropped her off in a hurry, saying

she had to go to work and she was already late enough, having been held up by the press camped up outside their door.

Suzie stared at Larkin and started picking at her flaking nail varnish. "Don't suppose there's any chance of a smoke?"

He pointed to the large No Smoking sign on the wall in front of her. She knew perfectly well, and he knew that she knew, but she was trying the edges. Reports of the fire had sickened him and the whole merry-go-round of press and media that surrounded this case, and the girl, was giving him a headache. It had started first thing this morning when he'd been called in to see the Superintendent.

"Larkin. I want you to handle this case personally. The media are making a fuss about this girl and if the press get a whisper that she is now a suspect they will go ballistic, worse still if it then turns out she's innocent after all. So I'm leaving it in your hands, Larkin, get it sorted before it blows up in our faces."

"Yes, Sir. No problem, Sir."

No problem? It had all the hallmarks of a big rotten tomato and it had fallen right into his lap. He knew the Superintendent's real worry was the interview for his big promotion, which was coming up next week. Nothing was allowed to get in the way of that.

Larkin suppressed his irritation and signalled to the WPC that the recorder should be turned on.

"Interview started 10.15am Tuesday 16th July in the presence of Mrs Henny, social worker for Miss Susanne Kelso."

"Do you know why you are here, today, Suzie?"

Suzie stared at Larkin, giving him the benefit of her scorn. "There was a fire and someone's put me up for starting it. You SO want to fix me up for this don't you? But read all about it! The papers say I'm ace. I saved that baby, didn't I?"

"Yes, you did, but let's talk about the fire for a moment. What can you tell me about it, or how it started?"

She rolled her eyes at him and said nothing.

"Suzie, you need to tell DI Larkin what happened." The social worker's voice was an irritating nasal moan, patronisingly coaxing. "Just tell the truth."

"And why don't you just shut up!" Suzie whined, in such an exact imitation of the woman's voice that the WPC behind her had to cough to suppress a laugh.

Mrs Henny flushed.

"Okay, enough!" Larkin growled. He looked the social worker straight in the eye and took great care to speak in a quiet, calm voice. "Mrs Henny, thank you. I'll take it from here."

He turned to Suzie, holding her gaze steadily for a few moments before he spoke. His voice was low and soft and he spoke to her as if there was no one else in the room. "If someone was going to start a fire, like the one last night, how do you think they would go about it?"

She looked down, pulled her chewing gum out of her mouth in two long strings and wound them round her finger before pushing them back between her teeth again. "How would I know?"

"Where were you when the fire started?"

"I dunno, do I?" Suzie stared straight at him, daring him to contradict her, but Larkin held her eyes and the silence grew, waiting for someone to fill it.

Suzie shifted in her seat. "I caught the baby, didn't I? Didn't say I wasn't out last night. Don't go putting words into my mouth. We were just muckin' about a bit and having a laugh when we heard the windows shattering and saw the smoke. Then she threw the baby out the window. Nearly wet myself when that happened."

DI Larkin looked down at his notes. "So, why do you think you were identified by a witness as one of two people she saw running away from the flats just before the fire?"

He waited a moment but she shrugged and said nothing.

"Why don't you tell me what happened last night?"

DON'T JUDGE ME

Suzie

It's not that I don't want to tell him the truth, part of me does, part of me wants to shock him, to make him look at me, not like a worm under his foot, or some kid that's trouble, but as a person, me, who I am — like he could actually understand that. Yeah. Right!

I don't really know why I did it. It was stupid, really, but I just wanted to do something. I didn't like the way she was treating Malky and we need to stick together, Malky and me, to look out for one another. You see, Malky and I are the same, not exactly the same but he's been in care, too, like me. We spent time in the same home a while back, except now he's back with his own mother, and I'm stuck with rubbish foster parents. They're not bad to me, exactly, but they never treat me the same as their own family. I'll always be an outsider, they're not my family.

So Malky and me need to stick together, because we understand each other, we've been through the same stuff.

I know he likes Jenna but she's just using him so I knew I had to do something about it. No one else would.

I didn't tell Jack, he wouldn't understand, would he?

CHAPTER 3

The night before

The solitary street light cast a yellowish haze over the crowd clustered on the street corner.

"Hey, Jack, where've you.... been?" Suzie staggered against Malky and draped her arm around his shoulder for support.

Jack crossed the road, slowly surveying the group, marking out who was there and who wasn't. He had been hoping Suzie would be there, she'd said she would come but he could never be sure with her, perhaps that was what attracted him, she was so unpredictable, dangerous. He knew his mother would never approve of him being with Suzie, so that was a plus to start with.

From what he could see she'd already had a few and was obviously well past her sell-by. Malky was pretty much holding her up and Jenna wasn't looking too happy about that.

Nothing new there then.

Suzie slid her arms from Malky's neck and stepped off the curb, tripping into Jack's arms. He could smell the cigarettes on her breath and see the drink-fuelled blurring of her eyes.

"You brought me something? Jack?" She patted his jacket but he pushed her hands away. "Think you've had enough, Suzie."

"Spoilsport!" She wobbled but failed to stand straight so she grabbed him again. "But I forgive you, you're my hero." She breathed in his face and he could hear the others laughing.

"She's wasted, mate," Sam shook his head. "Totally off her head."

"Am not!" Suzie slurred and tried to smooch at Jack but he dodged it. She started waving her arms and shouting at the top of her voice. "I am going to be famous and rich one day, then you'll be sorry, Sammy boy. When I'm a celebrity I can do anything I want and I won't speak to aa..any of you." She staggered over and the group made way for her until she reached Sam, wagging a finger in front of his face. "You'll sh.. eee."

Jack followed her. "Come on, Suzie."

She shrugged off his hands and batted them away as if he was an irritating fly. "No, I want to go and speak to my friend Malky. He'll be nice to me, won't you, Malky? "

Jack could see Jenna bristling. Malky's eyes flickered towards Jack. He looked like he didn't know what to do with Suzie when she was in this kind of mood, but Jack was pretty sure that Malky secretly liked the attention.

"Get your filthy paws off him," Jenna yelled at Suzie, her voice a spear of a shriek that pierced the night. "You little slag."

"Who're you calling a shh..lag?" Suzie launched herself at Jenna, grabbing at her carefully straightened curtain of jet black hair.

The crowd around them moved to give them some room as they set on each other shouting and screaming, pulling hair and scratching at each other's faces. Jack and Malky watched for a moment before moving in to separate them.

A woman leaned out of a window in the block of flats opposite. "Hey, you lot, clear off! My kids are trying to get to sleep. All of you. Go and fight somewhere else or I'll call the police."

With a new focus Suzie turned and swore at the woman but she had already closed her window and drawn the curtains.

"Stupid old bag. Who does she think she is. I'll get her."

"C'mon, Suzie. It's not worth it," Jack tried to turn her around, to take her away from the crowd.

"You couldn't 'get' your own grandmother, if you even knew who she was!" Jenna screamed at her.

Suzie slipped out of Jack's grasp and made for Jenna but the boys waded in and pulled them apart. Suzie shrugged Jack off but she wobbled and slipped off the curb.

As he pulled her to her feet again she noticed a young woman watching them from the pavement, a few yards away. She was just standing there staring, fear writing a shocked horror on her pale face.

"Wot you lookin' at?" Suzie had found a new focus for her anger. "Seen enough?"

The woman turned and ran.

CHAPTER 4

The Witness

The sound of her heels clacking against the pavement echoed loud and lonely in the darkness of the empty road. She thumped her heels against the concrete to make more noise. Was that more terrifying or reassuring? She couldn't decide. She concentrated on the sound, trying to ignore her fears before they left her crumpled and mewling on the street. She had looked at the trail of single streetlights that stood out, a lonely necklace of light, leading to a well-lit sanctuary. But how could it still be so far away?

The empty bus was not far behind, a safe haven in the darkness, but it wasn't totally empty, so she could never have stayed there.

It had all been going so well. She had been sitting on the bus, safe and unafraid, her route well planned beforehand. She had even been congratulating herself on how easy it was becoming to go out at night, until that sudden crunch and judder from the engine as the bus lurched to a stop in the middle of a dark stretch of road.

The driver had tried to restart the bus several times but the engine rumbled for a moment each time, trailing off to silence. The third time there was another nasty crash, and it went dead.

Through the dirt-streaked windows the housing estate just ahead had suggested a sanctuary of warm light and security.

The driver had been talking on his phone, obviously reporting the breakdown, but the few passengers left on the bus started shifting about in their seats.

"Sorry folks." He climbed out of his seat and stood at the front. "Looks like we're not going anywhere very fast. They're sending another bus but it may take a while."

Panic made a blur of the next few minutes. This wasn't in the plan. It wasn't meant to happen.

The couple sitting in front of her muttered to each other. "It's not that far, we might as well walk," the woman said. The man picked his two bags of shopping from the floor as he stood up and the woman followed him off the bus. One by one the other passengers got up and left.

They weren't meant to do that. They weren't meant to leave her alone. Safety, a feeling of security in numbers, that's what Dr Hopper always told her. But soon she was the only one left apart from the driver.

Alone with a strange man. It wasn't right; it wasn't part of the plan. She couldn't stay but the other option was not much better. What could she do?

Even if he stayed sitting in his own little driver's cab, he might get up again. The last of the passengers were disappearing, walking away from her and she could see them leaving the safe brightness cast by the interior lights of the bus. First their heads vanished, then their bodies and finally their heels were smothered by the darkness as they walked away from her, leaving her alone with the driver.

It wasn't right.

The well-lit buildings far ahead looked welcoming, and in the haze of fear she suddenly recognised where she was. It wasn't far from her stop. She could walk it, couldn't she? That's it! She could walk to the lights.

She could do it. She had to.

"You sure, you don't want to wait here, lass?" the driver asked, as she stepped down tentatively onto the pavement. "They shouldn't be too long."

She shook her head, hardly able to shape the words. She

wasn't sure if she could speak to him at all. She had to keep strong and she definitely couldn't change her mind, not now that she had used up all her courage and stepped off the bus. He looked a kind enough man, but nothing could have persuaded her to get back on again. He might try to talk to her, then he might come closer to chat, and she would be alone with him, trapped, unable to get away.

Frightening scenarios filled her head. However unlikely they were, the thought of what might happen - what could happen — threatened to smother her until the panic would render her a quivering useless wreck. She had to hold onto the plan; that was the only way to survive.

"Thanks, I like to walk. It's not far." She told the lie very smoothly and convincingly, she thought.

One step. The paving under her feet was still bathed in the light from the bus but the next step would take her into darkness.

Eyes front, keep looking at the lights, she told herself. They would get closer and closer with each step. Another step, another and then another, until the only sound in her head was the clacking of her heels on the pavement.

It's not far, it's not far. It's not far...

She kept up the mantra in her head, blocking out all other thoughts, focusing on the next step and then one following that, trying to ignore the darkness. Her eyes staring straight ahead, looking longingly at the warmth of the lights around the housing estate, the safety of bright lights. It was the dark she couldn't stand.

The sheer relief of reaching the first of the streetlights meant she'd made it. She'd been lost in her thoughts on the bus, a technique developed to help her face going anywhere in the evening, in the darkness, on her own.

It was all still too new, this courage she had found, to go out on her own. For a long time she had stayed at home, never venturing out because there was no one she trusted. Trust, that was the issue. Who can you trust? You can't trust anyone, can you?

Slowly she had started going out more, but Dr Hopper, her counsellor, had suggested that she was getting better and now she might try going out in the evening. Suggesting ways to create confidence, ways to fight back against the fear. Telling her she had to act herself, not wait to let others dictate her actions.

She had taken the advice to heart, starting with small everyday decisions. Taking control of her life, probably for the first time, making plans and following them through rigidly, with no half measures.

It worked well, giving her a kind of strength and power she had never known before. But tonight everything had gone wrong and she could feel the familiar crushing fear hovering at the edge of her mind. Beneath it was a cold anger that all her careful plans were in danger of going awry.

But she kept going, walking, moving; trying not to think about it; trying not to let the crippling fear take hold. She knew she had to take control, just like she'd been told to do. It wasn't far now. She was almost there.

That was when she saw the crowd of kids. Not really kids; most of them were taller than her five feet and one inch. She wasn't all that much older than them, but if you believed the press they all got drunk or were on drugs and carried knives or baseball bats, some even had swords or guns. She hated crowds, and a crowd of teenagers, youths, hoodies, that was terrifying.

They were all dangerous, weren't they?

Was that ridiculous? But she had reason to know that some of them were.

She never used to believe all that. When she was younger, when she lived at home and everything was fine and she was carefree and happy. That was before, before it happened. Her father would never have hurt anyone. The familiar anger rose from the pit of her stomach, turning to bitterness in her mouth. It wasn't fair.

She used to think they couldn't all be bad, could they? But now she wasn't so sure.

She remembered the days afterwards. The worry and the loss; that aching, hollow feeling and then came the fear, the mind numbing terror of being alone.

No! She wasn't going to think about it! Not going to think about it at all. Had to think of something else, anything else. To take control, hold onto a goal and not let go of it. She would start by thinking about walking. The next step, and the next one. She counted her steps one by one.

She wouldn't look at them messing about on the street corner, spilling out carelessly onto the road.

Ignore them.

They were making a lot of noise with their hard voices. Some had hoods pulled up to cover their faces but she could imagine what was behind the hoods, the hard, uncaring faces, the mocking eyes. She felt vulnerable, exposed and she could sense a blind terror hovering within her.

"No!" the word slipped from her mouth, an unbidden whisper. "Not going to think about it. Not going to let it take control. I'll be fine, I'll be in control, just to need to get past them."

That was when the girls started fighting. She shuddered and stopped, mesmerised by the violence, the noise. Two of the boys were trying to separate them but the girls were like animals, one blonde and one dark, snarling at each other and fighting to get back into the fight. Claws for hands, teeth bared between insults and screams.

A window in the flats above was thrown open, a woman hurled threats, shocking them into silence for a moment.

The focus changed and the blonde girl glared up at the woman with her own threats, but the window was closed now. Obviously drunk, or on drugs, the blonde swayed in the arms of the boy who had been holding her back from the fight.

That was when the girl turned and noticed her standing there, watching them.

"Wot you lookin' at?" The girl's face snarled as she spat out the words.

"Come, on, Suzie, that's enough." The boy tried to turn her around but she pulled away from him.

"Seen enough?" The girl grabbed her top and yanked it up. The boys all whooped and whistled.

Trapped by the girl's dark blue eyes and defiant stare, she was welded to the ground by fear and embarrassment, unable to run but terrified to stay. She felt a surge of primal fear, familiar in its terror. She had vowed it would never happen to her again, she would never be this frightened or powerless and afraid but here she was unable to breathe, unable to move. Like prey trapped by a hunter.

The horror triggered something deep inside her. She felt it grow, cold and dark, striving to take over, to take control. It was swamped by her paralysing fear but there was a tendril of strength, just enough to grab and hold onto, to shatter the lock of terror that held her.

She turned and ran.

CHAPTER 5

Jack's grandmother followed the young WPC into the room where DI Larkin was sitting behind a desk writing up his notes.

"This is Jack Sorley, and Mrs Bell, his grandmother, Sir."

"What a tiny room." Jack's grandmother frowned as she settled herself into one of the two chairs and let her huge handbag collapse onto the floor beside her. It spread like a gelatinous lump of multicoloured cloth. "I'll have a cup of tea, dear. Earl Grey, mind, with two sugars, please."

"Gran!" Jack thought he would die of embarrassment.

Gran was always taking charge of things in what seemed like a gentle, quiet manner but she usually got what she wanted. In some ways she was just like his mother, controlling but putting a smiling face on it, as if they hoped no one would notice. Jack hated it when they both did that, but for some reason it never seemed quite so irritating when it was Gran.

Larkin turned to the WPC. "A good idea. Jenny, would you mind getting us a couple of cups of tea?"

"Yes, Sir, right away."

"And perhaps a soft drink for you, Jack?"

Jack nodded.

As the door closed behind her, Larkin sat looking at Jack for a moment. Jack was uncomfortable, embarrassed by his grandmother, but it was more than that. He stared around the room as the silence stretched, his facial muscles working hard to keep control.

Larkin spoke for the recording. "Interview with Jack Sorley — interview started 11.45pm.

"All right, Son, why don't you tell me what you remember about last night."

"It wasn't us. You need to believe me. I would never..." He

hesitated and swallowed. The words had dried up in his throat. "I would never..." He stopped, silent for a moment, trapped by the words and an image of smouldering cloth. He took a deep breath. "You have to believe me. I...We...we didn't do it!"

Sitting opposite him Larkin said nothing. Jack hung his head and brushed his hair out of his eyes with the back of his hand.

His grandmother looked concerned. "He's a good boy, Mr... what was it?"

"Detective Inspector Larkin." Larkin smiled at her. "I'm sure Jack is a good boy, Mrs Bell, but I need him to tell me what he saw last night."

He turned back to Jack. "This is a very serious affair, Jack. Someone started that fire and people are in hospital, they might die. We've had an eyewitness account that puts you in the area around the time the fire was set. Can you start by telling me where you were from about 6pm last night? Work your way forward."

Jack cleared his throat several times before speaking. "I met up with everyone at the corner of Station Road about half six-ish, I'm not sure what time it was. I'd said I would meet up with Malky and some of the others."

"What did you have planned?"

He shook his head. "Nothing, really, we were just going to hang out; see what came up."

"And when you arrived...?" Larkin prompted him.

"I was a bit later because my mum had phoned. She's away in New York, she's always away working on some story or other. I waited to see..." He stopped and cleared his throat. "It was a waste of time, she didn't want to speak to me, anyway. When I arrived everyone was there already, but nothing much was happening."

"Were you expecting to meet up with Suzie?"

"Yeah, she said she'd be there, but you can never be sure with Suzie."

"Were you all drinking?"

His grandmother pursed her lips but Larkin raised his hand slightly to forestall any comment. Jack avoided eye contact with her.

"Some of them were. When I got there some of the others had some cans, and someone had a half bottle of vodka, I think."

"Was Suzie drinking? Was she drunk, or more than that?"

"Naw, Suzie doesn't do drugs, she was just a bit drunk, not smashed or totally off her head or anything, but she was pretty well on."

"Had you arranged to do anything particular that night, you and Suzie?"

"Not really, it wasn't anything definite like that. I just wanted to see her again. She and I, well, I wanted to see her, that's all. It was just where everyone hangs out, everyone knows that."

"So what happened next?"

"We just hung about for a bit. Suzie always acts up when she's off her face and she was making a bit of a fuss."

"What kind of thing was she doing?"

"She started getting mouthy, saying lots of stuff. Most of it was out of order, but everyone knows she gets like that, so no one takes any notice."

"But someone did take notice that night, didn't they?"

He shrugged. "Suppose so."

"So what happened?"

He started picking at the edge of the desk and the room echoed as he tapped his heel on the floor in a disjointed beat. The detective ignored it, his face betraying no emotion, refusing to let the noise distract him.

"There was this woman, she was walking towards us. She was on her own and she stopped when she saw us and just stood there, staring. She should have just kept going but she stopped and stared at Suzie and Jenna. They were having a bit of a fight. Her standing there just staring and not moving, well, it was totally weird and it just made Suzie worse."

"What did Suzie do?"

Jack shrugged. "Nothing much, she probably just said something. I don't remember. She probably just ranted a bit at the woman."

"What did the woman do?"

"She muttered something. I didn't hear what it was she said, but a minute later she turned and ran off as if something was chasing her. Total nutter, really. We all just laughed."

"So did anything else happen that night?"

"No, that was it, until we saw the fire...I don't think we believed what we were seeing. We all just stood watching it happen and then at the last moment Suzie ran forward and caught the kid."

He started tapping his foot against the desk again. "That was it, really. Can I go now?"

The door opened and the WPC brought in the tea.

"Ah, thank you, Jenny."

Jack's grandmother took her cup of tea, sipped it and made a face. Then she smiled at the WPC. "Thank you, dear, shame you didn't have any Earl Grey though." She turned to Larkin. "That young girl was in the papers, all about her catching the baby, an' all. Wasn't that a little miracle."

"Indeed it was, Mrs Bell. We're almost done here, Jack. Just a couple more questions." Larkin was watching the boy. "You're sure there wasn't anything else? Did something else happen that night?"

"No, nothing really." Jack had been tapping his foot against the table and he stopped suddenly. Silence filled the room, louder than any noise, until his grandmother picked up her cup and slurped her tea, loudly.

Larkin shuffled some papers and found the one he was looking for. "You and Suzie left the group before the fire started. Where did you go?"

Jack shook his head rapidly. "When Suzie and Jenna started fighting we all knew we had to get them separated. So I took Suzie away to let her cool down and try to get her sobered up a bit.

'Don't know what she'd been drinking but just after we walked away from the rest she started being sick. It took a bit to get her sorted and when we came back around the corner the building was on fire."

"You know Jenna, don't you?"

"Yeah, course!"

"Did you know that the flat where the fire started belonged to Jenna's family?"

Jack nodded.

"Luckily the family was away at the time and there was no one there. Do you think Suzie knew where Jenna lived?"

"Of course she knows where Jenna lives, we all do. Why are you trying to make out it was Suzie? We were nowhere near it. We'd never do anything like that. Is that what you're saying?"

Jack jumped up from his seat and leaned forwards, gripping onto the edge of the desk, as if he wanted to tip it over. His knuckles turned white with the pressure. "Is that it? You think we did it? Don't you?"

The WPC moved towards him but Larkin waved her away.

"Just calm down, Son. Sit down! No one is saying anything."

"I'm not your son! And you can't pin this on us. We weren't, we... we weren't anywhere near the place."

"I have a witness who saw you and Suzie coming out of the entrance to the flats just before the fire broke out. Can you explain that?"

"I told you, Suzie was feeling sick so we went round to the park benches, they're not far from the front of the flats. But whoever your witness is, they're wrong, it wasn't us. You have to believe me, we couldn't do anything like that."

"Did you see anyone coming in or out of the flats while you were there?"

"I would have told you if I had, wouldn't I?"

"Okay, Jack, let's leave it like that for now but I will probably need to speak to you again. But if you remember anything else about what happened you must come and tell me. Okay?"

CHAPTER 6

When they left the Police station Gran patted Jack's hand. "What a nice man that policeman was. It was a terrible thing that fire, but I knew you wouldn't have had anything to do with it. You're a good boy, Jack. I told your mother that very thing when I spoke to her on the phone. You just need to tell the policeman if you remember anything else."

"Sure, Gran," Jack mumbled.

"Now, I just need to go and collect my paper."

Jack's mobile rang as they arrived at the newsagents. He signalled to his grandmother that he would wait for her outside.

"Jack, can you talk?"

"Yup, Suzie, what's up?"

"Where are you? Have the police spoken to you yet?"

"Yeah, just left them. They seem to think we had something to do with the fire."

"I know. I think they're trying to set us up for it. They had me in first thing this morning. What did you tell them? Go AWAY, eff off! I said, NO!"

"*What*?"

"No, not you, Jack. It's these reporters they keep coming up to me and asking me questions. They're camped out outside my foster parents' house, which is not going down well at all. You know how much they think I'm trouble and they're getting really pissed off and making out that it's all my fault that the press are here. So I left the house, but they keep trying to follow me.

"I need to see you, now, Jack. Did you hear that they're saying the fire must have started in Jenna's flat?"

"Yeah, Malky told me."

"One of the reporters told me. Asked if I knew anyone who had a grudge against her, or her family."

"What did you tell them, Suzie?"

"How would I know who had a grudge against them? Anyway, I wouldn't tell that lot if their hair was on fire!"

"Where are you now?"

"At the end of Simpson Road, heading towards Well Street."

"Right. Go into the Mall and I'll meet you there, in five minutes. At the north end."

"OK. But Jack..."

"What?"

"Don't be long."

"I won't, Suzie. I'll see you there."

DON'T JUDGE ME
Jack

I was glad to get out of the Police station and I just hoped that Gran wasn't going to start asking loads of questions but thankfully, she didn't. I wish I lived in a normal house and didn't have to live with Gran so much of the time, but that's Mum's fault, she's never here.

Gran started talking as soon as we left. Even though I never said a word back to her, she just went on "Nah Nah..." but Gran never seems to need anyone to join in her conversation, she just goes on and on, answering her own questions as soon as she asks them. At least it meant I could tune her out and try to get things straight in my head.

I knew that Mum would be arriving back from New York in a couple of days and she'd go bananas when she heard they had someone who'd said I had been involved in the fire. She would totally crack up if I ended up in the papers. I could see the headlines. "ARSON — Top journalist's son under suspicion." But then, that was all she cared about, whether I did something to harm her precious reputation. Part of me liked the idea. I was furious with her and it would serve her right, but just now she wasn't so much the problem as Suzie.

I'd told the detective that we'd been together all the time, but of course that wasn't entirely true.

Suzie had been feeling cold, so I'd left her to go and get her jacket.

"I think I put it down on the low wall at the front of the flats, beside where we were all standing," she'd said. "Can you get it for me?"

Everyone else had gone by then but I couldn't find her jacket at first so it took me a while. Eventually I discovered it tucked down behind the wall, but what I can't remember is just how long it took to find the jacket and get back to where I'd left Suzie in the park by the flats. Ten minutes? Fifteen?

When I got back to the bench where I'd left her, it was empty, but when I decided I should go and look for her, she came walking towards me. I can still see it in my head. She had just stepped out of the main door to the flats — and she was smiling. That gave me a real scare. Why was she smiling like that? What had she been doing? What did she know?

It made no sense at all. I wasn't about to ask, and Suzie wasn't saying much either. I had no idea why she'd been in there or what she had been doing. There had to be an explanation, it was just that I couldn't think of one and part of me didn't want to ask, in case I didn't like the answer.

CHAPTER 7

Suzie hung around the jewellery stall at the far end of the Mall. She was trying on a couple of fancy rings until the stall owner glared at her for the third time. She was about to give him a mouthful of abuse when she spotted Jack coming towards her. With a flourish she pulled the last two rings off her finger and tossed them into a large pile of necklaces.

She was irritated that the stall owner automatically assumed she wasn't going to buy them. Okay, so she wasn't, but he didn't know that and the way he looked at her, she knew he thought she was going to steal them.

Jack walked up beside her but she turned, heading away from him further into the Mall, without saying a word. He followed until she slumped onto a bench in the middle of the thoroughfare. She sat silently for a moment or two twisting the bangles on her wrist.

She turned to face him. "What did the police say? What did you tell them? Did they ask you about me?"

Jack shrugged. "He just wanted to know what I'd seen, what we were all doing last night. He told me someone had said they saw us coming out of the flats, but that's not right." He looked straight at her, searching her face for a reaction. "Because I wasn't there, was I?"

He left the question hanging in the air, the implication heavy between them. Suzie looked away and started playing with a thin strand of her hair, twisting it and rolling it between her finger and thumb until she was holding it close to the end. She began jabbing the short ends against her skin. It felt like tiny, sharp needles. The small red mark at the edge of her eye showed that it was a familiar, comforting, almost instinctive response whenever she was worried. "So, what did you tell them?"

"I told them what happened. What do you think I told them?"

"Did you tell them we were together all the time?" Suzie began chewing on the nail of her little finger, edgy, watching him. She could see he was annoyed that she wasn't telling him anything, but that was too bad for him. She didn't need to tell anyone anything, did she.

Jack looked away. "I told them the witness was wrong, and that we didn't see anyone coming out of the flats."

Suzie relaxed, sitting back against the seat and stretching her legs out in front of her.

"What did you tell them, Suzie?"

"Not much."

She got up and started walking away. Jack shook his head but he got up to follow her.

"Yo! Jack, hey. Jack... Suzie!"

Jack turned around and saw Malky and Jenna coming up behind them. He turned to see if Suzie had stopped too. She was staring at Jenna, but she waited until they caught up.

"You been in to speak with the Bizzies yet?"

Jack grinned and shook his head, "No one calls them that any more, Malky, you daft prat!"

Malky shrugged. "We've to go and speak to them this afternoon. Jenna's to go in first, haven't you, Doll?"

"Don't call me 'Doll', Malky, you know I hate it."

Suzie tried unsuccessfully to hide a smile. Jenna was always trying to be a bit above the rest of them but she wasn't looking so sure of herself this morning. "Do they know who did it yet, Jenna?"

Jack was watching Suzie but Suzie was staring at Jenna.

Slumped against the railing, Jenna looked down at the

shoppers on the level below. She pulled out a tissue and began dabbing at the corners of her eyes, carefully avoiding her mascara. "Everything we have is ruined, all my clothes and the house, everything! Never thought what it would be like, a fire. And poor Mrs Harper... and her baby." She started sobbing into her tissue. "At least you saved the baby, Suzie."

Suzie looked at a loss, she wasn't used to Jenna losing control, or being nice to her. People were starting to turn and stare at them. "Let's go and get a coffee," she said and turned away heading towards Joe's, their favourite café.

"Mine's a latte, Jack," Suzie said, as she went to the back to grab an empty table. Jenna followed her and sat down while Jack and Malky went to get their drinks.

"Was everything destroyed in the fire?" Suzie asked, as casually as she could manage. She was never sure how Jenna would react to anything she said so Suzie wasn't about to give her the chance.

But Jenna just nodded. "Absolutely everything. We have nothing left at all. My mother is so upset, especially as we have to stay with my aunt. Mum and her sister don't get on at all."

"Have the police told you who they think did it?"

Jenna sniffed again. "No, they were asking if we had any enemies or if we'd had any racial attacks or threats recently. But they did say there was a witness and they were 'following several lines of enquiry', whatever that really means."

Jack arrived at the table with their drinks. "They told me they had a witness, too, but I'm not sure about that because if they did, why haven't they arrested someone?"

Malky sat down and leaned forward, his voice a harsh whisper. "Did they tell you who the witness was, and what they saw?" He was looking around to see if anyone was close enough to hear.

Jack shrugged, he wasn't about to say the police thought it was him and Suzie. He could see Suzie's cold stare from the corner of his eye, warning him to say nothing. As if he needed any warning. His stomach churned, he didn't want to think about it any more.

"There probably isn't any witness at all," Malky said, and started to mimic the detective in one of his silly voices. "'We have a witness but it's a three-eyed alien, so we can't tell anyone.'"

Suzie laughed and even Jenna managed a smile.

"They do that all the time," he said, getting a moustache of milk on his top lip as he took a drink of his coffee. "It's a favourite police tactic. They try to make suspects confess to something by pretending they have a witness." Malky sat back into his seat. "As if that would work! It doesn't matter anyway, they'll never catch them."

Jenna was looking at him strangely.

"What?" he snapped at her. "They never do, except in films. Criminals are just too clever!"

Jenna shook her head and looked at him silently for a moment. "I can't believe you think everything is all such a joke, Malky." She turned away from him, taking out a mirror to check her face and wiping the smudge of mascara from her eyes and then she took out her lip gloss and started reapplying it carefully.

"What?" Malky barked into the silence. "Just trying to lighten the mood, that's all. What's the matter with you lot?" He gulped at his drink.

Jenna carefully smudged her lips together making her lip gloss glisten. "If you don't know..." She narrowed her eyes at him. "It sounds as if you think it's all just a joke and you don't want them to find out who did it."

"Everyone knows the police are like that," he snapped back at her. His face flushed and he crumpled his empty can in one hand. "I've heard them do that on the TV. They make it up when they don't know. They're not supposed to do it but they do. Happens in all the best films when they just fit someone up for it, someone that suits them. That's all I meant."

Jenna ducked her head down, letting her sheet of straight black hair fall across her face. "This is not a film, Malky. It's real." She picked up her shoulder bag and got up. "I'd better go. My Dad said he'd meet me at the end of the High Street."

"I'll walk you part of the way," Malky offered.

Jenna shook her head. "Probably better if you don't. Dad knows I'm here and he might start walking up to meet me."

Jenna could see that he wasn't happy but he had really annoyed her when he had started making out it didn't matter. She had so many things going round in her head just now. She had to get things straight and Malky fooling around just wasn't helping.

As soon as Jenna had gone, Malky stood up. "See ya later, I've got things to do."

Jack watched him heading in the opposite direction to Jenna, hands stuffed into his pockets as he slouched off. Malky was normally the joker but he was obviously angry with Jenna, especially after the remark about her father. That always got to him. But Jack was glad he'd gone, he needed time to speak to Suzie alone. To find out what she knew.

They left the café and Jack walked her home. He wanted to ask her why she had been in the flats and what she'd seen, but Suzie kept steering the conversation away from the previous night. By the time they got to her house Suzie was laughing and chatting as if she hadn't a care in the world and Jack hadn't managed to find out anything.

There were a couple of reporters still waiting outside but he glared at them and pushed Suzie past, telling them she had nothing to say. One was more aggressive than the rest and thrust a microphone in their faces.

She asked if Jack and Suzie knew it was arson, and did they know who had started the fire? Jack pushed her out of the way and they ran towards the front door.

Suzie closed the door behind them and leaned back against it.

"Has it been like that all the time?"

Suzie grinned. "That was nothing, there were at least fifteen of them yesterday!"

"I guess you don't have a back door?"

She shook her head.

"Is that you, Suzie?" A voice shouted from the kitchen.

"That's my foster mother, Penny," Suzie whispered, rolling her eyes. "She's a real pain!.

"Yes, it's me. Jack's here, too." Suzie shouted back.

A tall, thin woman came to the door of the kitchen. Jack thought her face looked as if a smile had never passed within a mile of it. There were deep creases holding her mouth down at the corners, producing a permanently grumpy expression. But then Suzie had told him she rarely smiled.

"There's someone here to speak to you, both of you."

Curious, they entered the kitchen but Jack stopped at the doorway. "*Mum?* What are you doing here?"

DON'T JUDGE ME

Suzie

I don't care. I wanted to do it. Jenna deserved it, didn't she? Anyway it doesn't matter now, except that it would've shown them all and sorted Jenna out. At least that was what I thought, but now it all seems a bit petty. I've never seen her look so unsure of herself as she did at the Mall today. Heck, she even said something okay about me. She's obviously not herself!

Jack would have stopped me doing it if he'd known, that's why I've not told him. He's too good, doesn't like upsetting people, regular Mr Perfect. If I'd told him what I'd done he'd just look at me that way he does. He's like that, always trying to make me do things right, looking out for me. I know he's desperate to ask me what I was doing at the flats and I can't tell him, so I keep distracting him. Not sure it will work much longer. Jack isn't really hard enough, but I think I like that about him, not that I'd ever tell him that.

Anyway, it would have shown Jenna that I don't wimp out and make empty threats and... and... that NOTHING bothers me. Except sometimes, when I think about the little kids and their mother stuck in hospital. Life's rubbish, but anyway, I saved the baby, little Leila.

Look, I'm not off my head or anything like that, I know that's not her name, that she's not my baby sister, but I can't think of her as anything else. I almost didn't want to give her to the policewoman after the fire. I just wanted to hold her, to keep her safe. At least she has someone who cares what happens to her.

I suppose this is just another thing that will make my foster parents keen to get rid of me as soon as they can. They don't keep me anywhere long and I know she hates me anyway, they always do. I'm just a way for them to earn some extra cash. I've no idea where they'll send me next. It could be anywhere and I'm not sure I care. It might be another care home but I hope not, having foster parents is only a bit better than those kids' homes I was in before. Sometimes I used to wish I could have had proper parents, someone to adopt me, someone who wanted me but that was when I was younger and believed in that kind of thing. But no one wanted me.

Anyway, they can't make me do anything I don't want to. Even when I was little they could never make me do anything if I decided not to. I learned that early on, I had to.

Last night, when Jack took me away from the crowd, I said I was feeling sick. I wasn't really and I tried to pull him into the bushes for a quick snog, but he said I was too drunk and suddenly I did start to feel sick. So I told him I was cold and I needed my jacket. Of course he went to get it for me. I knew he would.

He never hesitated a moment and left me sitting on the bench giving me time to get the deed done before he got back, except he was quicker than I thought and he came back just as I stepped out of the door of the flats. I could see a question in his eyes, just as it was on the way back from the Mall today. So I did the same as I did today, I started talking about other things until the moment passed and he was distracted.

CHAPTER 8

Jenna followed her father into the interview room and sat down beside him. He was wearing a suit borrowed from her aunt, one that had belonged to her uncle before he died. He looked a bit strange because it was too tight and straining at the buttons. Her mum had tried to persuade him to leave the jacket open but he had insisted that it wasn't proper. So he sat there looking hot and uncomfortable. It brought it home to her how difficult this was for all of them. Her father, normally an ebullient but cheery personality, was subdued and seemed diminished in the bleak dull room.

He took her hand and she was grateful for the comfort, but her brain was working furiously trying to decide what she could and couldn't say. She couldn't bear to upset her father when he was like this. Avoiding speaking about Malky at home and telling little white lies about who she was spending time with seemed so much easier than this bald-faced lying to a stranger, worse still a policeman. She'd never been in a police station before and it was intimidating, all the official language they used just made it worse.

The detective came into the room and shook hands with her father.

"Mr Chowdhury, I'm Detective Inspector Larkin. Thank you for bringing Jenna in to speak to me today. I appreciate that your family have been through a lot but I am sure you will realise how important it is to get to the bottom of this and find out what happened."

"Certainly, I too need to know who has wanted to do this terrible thing to my family. We were very, very sad to hear about Mrs Harper and her children. They are good neighbours."

DI Larkin nodded. "I will be wanting to take a statement

from you later, Mr Chowdhury, but right now I want to ask Jenna a few questions about what she saw last night."

Her father looked at her and gave a reassuring smile as he patted her hand. "She's a good girl, my Jenna. I know she will tell you anything she knows, but she was with us most of the night. We were celebrating my nephew's birthday. It was a big family occasion and Jenna was there with us, but she was not feeling well and went home early. When we heard about the fire we were terrified that Jenna might have been at home when it happened."

Jenna felt her insides twist and curdle and for a moment she wondered if she was going to be sick. She took a breath and forced a lame smile on her face for her father's benefit, struggling to keep the nausea from taking over.

DI Larkin looked down at his papers and then looked up at her.

"Jenna can you just begin by telling me where you were when the fire started?"

She frowned, this wasn't the question she had been expecting. What could she say? The silence grew and her brain was whirling round in circles.

"Jenna?" Her father was looking at her. "Answer the detective."

She had to say something.

"I don't know?" As soon as the words were out she knew it sounded pretty pathetic. "I mean, how could I know? I don't know when the fire started."

"Okay, Jenna, why not tell me about last night. You were out with your family and you left. What time was that?"

"I left about seven-ish, I think. I went straight home. It wasn't far so I got there just after that."

"Did you go home alone?"

Jenna nodded. "Mum was going to go with me but I knew she wanted to stay at the party, so I walked back by myself."

"But you didn't stay at home?"

She glanced at her father and bit her lower lip. "No. I'd been feeling unwell but by the time I got home I felt better. I think getting out into the fresh air helped."

"So when did you leave the house?

Jenna shrugged. "Not sure. It wasn't long after that. I got changed and then I remembered that some of my friends were going to be meeting up on the corner, so I went out to see if they were there."

"Did you see anyone hanging around the flats when you came out?"

Her heart started hammering, was he going to ask about Malky? "My cousins! They came to the flat but they were only there for a moment or two then they left. They were late and should have been at the party. Then I left too. Look, I never saw anything. If I had, don't you think I would have said?"

"Jenna!" Her father's voice was soft but reproachful. "Be polite."

She looked down at her hands and started playing with the ring Malky had given her, twisting it round and round her thumb.

"Jenna, it's very important that we find out everything we can about last night. People could have died because someone set fire to your flat. We need to make sure this doesn't happen again."

"I'm sorry. But I didn't see anything."

"Okay. Why don't you tell me what happened between you and Suzie. You had an argument, what was it about?"

Jenna felt her heart start to race again, there was so much she couldn't say in front of her father and she hoped the policeman wouldn't drop her in it.

"I... It was nothing." Jenna struggled to find something she could say. "She'd been drinking and was being stupid. It wasn't anything really. We just don't get on much."

"Do you think she would have a reason to want to harm you, or your family?"

"Suzie? No, we don't get on but she'd never do anything like that."

"What about the others that were there? Had you arranged to meet up with them? What about Jack... and Malky? Would they have known your family was away from home that night?"

Her father was still, she could feel his stillness radiating like a physical thing towards her. He was waiting to hear her say she never spent time with them. She knew he hated Malky and had told her she was to stay away from him. She wanted to lie, and say she never saw them, but that they might have been there. The words wouldn't come out and the longer she was silent the worse it was getting.

The words burst out in a gush. "They're just part of the crowd. We all hang out together. I don't know much about them or what they know. You'd have to ask them."

She could hear the lie crumble in the air in front of her and knew her father would have some hard questions when they got home. She kept her eyes fixed on the table.

DI Larkin consulted his notes. "Just a couple more questions, Jenna. When the crowd dispersed, before the fire started, where did you go?"

On safer ground she relaxed a bit. "I went round to Blueson's, the newsagents, with Katy and Liz. They wanted to get something to drink, some Coke. When we heard all the noise, the glass shattering and the screaming, the sirens. We ran back and everyone was standing outside the flat. It was horrible. That was when Mrs Harper screamed and... and threw her baby out of the window." Jenna's eyes filled and she began to cry softly.

Larkin and her father exchanged glances and Larkin nodded. "That's all for now, Jenna. Mr Chowdhury, I may want to speak to you and Jenna again, tomorrow, but someone will call you and let you know when."

"Of course. We are at your disposal." Her father stood up and shook hands with DI Larkin before escorting Jenna out of the room.

DON'T JUDGE ME

Jenna

I keep going over last night in my mind, what happened and if I could have done something to make things turn out differently. Nothing ever works out the way you expect and all my plans went up in smoke, well, perhaps they were all messed up and wouldn't have worked out anyway. Everything's ruined, all my stuff, I've got nothing left and Mum keeps crying all the time.

When the policeman started asking me questions I had to be really careful what I said. With Dad there I could hardly say anything about Malky, what a nightmare!

It wasn't easy getting away from the party and I had to plead with my mother again and again. She thought I should stay, especially because Pavan was only there so that he could meet me. Size me up more like. I felt as if I was in a cattle market with his mother and father, and his sister looking me over, I wanted to ask if they would like to open my mouth and count my teeth! I could imagine his mother telling him I had good childbearing hips and would give him many sons.

It makes me so angry. It makes the fury bubble up inside me, like hot lava waiting to erupt. I hate them all.

I almost felt sorry for Pavan, but not really, He seemed to be going along with it all far too happily. I would almost have forgiven him if he had been bright enough to agree with me about how horrible it all was. But he doesn't look all that smart, whatever my father thinks. His parents run their small empire as though it was Tesco's and I feel like the bargain of the week, but they like the idea that my parents come from a good family. I know it gives them respectability and status among their friends, but why do I have to be the one who pays the price?

Mum told me ages ago that she and Dad met only once before they got married and her parents had chosen Dad to be her husband. They seem to be happy but I just want to be able to fall in love with someone and marry them because they love me, is it too much to ask? To be able to choose the person I live with all the rest of my life? About two seconds after meeting Pavan I was pretty sure he would be the last person I wanted to marry. He's just...ugh!

I finally managed to persuade my mother that I was feeling sick. (I couldn't very well tell her it was Pavan that was making me feel that way, could I? At least not in front of his parents!) My aunt was smiling at them and they were all talking as if it was a business deal, as if it was all final and decided but no one had asked me what I thought. I felt sick, and trapped. I could see my whole life crumbling in front of my eyes. This was not what I had imagined it would be like.

So I told my mother that it was that time of the month and I needed to go home. She volunteered to come with me but I said I would be fine and made sure she was kept busy with Pavan's mother so that I could slip away.

All the way home the unfairness of it all was bubbling up like acid in my stomach. I ran most of the way and it was probably as I was running that I decided. I had to make sure it was all ready, that it would work and I really needed to get into some reasonable clothes before I met up with Malky. He hates me wearing anything that isn't really modern, and that doesn't mean the traditional outfit my father had decided I should wear to meet Pavan's family. We'd had a bit of an argument about that before we went to the party but I knew I was not going to win.

By the time I had it all sorted I had to run down the road to meet Malky, but it was already quite late and everyone else was there, except Jack. He came across the street just after I arrived. Just as well because that bitch Suzie had started making out with Malky. She always throws herself at Malky and she was well wasted already. I don't know what Jack sees in her.

When she saw Jack she stumbled over and fell into his arms. A few moments later she came back over to Malky and started wrapping herself around him again.

I was ready to slap her, and I expected Malky to shove her away but he didn't, which made me boiling mad. I was fuming.

It had been a horrible evening, all that stuff with Pavan and his family and then when I saw my cousins outside the flats I started to panic. What were they doing there? I was in such a state that I didn't know what to do and ended up leaving my bag behind and I couldn't go back for it, could I? Everything was going wrong, so I really didn't need her coming on to Malky like that. I just lost it.

I'm not proud of myself, but it was all too much, I just flipped. I grabbed her hair and started screaming at her. Jack hauled her off me and Malky grabbed my waist at the same time. Just then Mrs Harper from the top floor, stuck her head out the window and told us to go away and stop waking her kids.

I hid behind Malky so she wouldn't see me and tell my mother but Suzie gave her a mouthful. Then that woman walked up towards us and just stood there, staring. Suzie said something and whatever it was the woman suddenly turned and ran off as if she was terrified. Suzie just laughed.

Jack took Suzie away after that but I was so angry with Malky that I told him what I thought of him and stormed off. I was furious that he let Suzie kiss him like that but he seemed to think I was over-reacting. He says he loves me, but then he always says that and I don't know what that means any more. So I went off with Katy and Liz to the corner shop for smokes. I don't smoke, but it was just an excuse to walk away from Malky, so that he knew how angry I was.

He had ruined everything.

CHAPTER 9

DI Larking watched Malcolm Norwell and his mother come into the room. The boy looked like your normal teenager, a little scruffy around the edges and that sullen look which was no surprise. His mother was the opposite, tall and slim with a slightly toothy grin and eager-to-please expression. With her long slender neck and over made up eyes, when she smiled at Larkin he had a sudden image of a cartoon giraffe with a big-lipped smile and huge eyelashes.

Trying to banish the picture in his head he indicated that they should sit down. The boy's mother fussed at him to take his hands out of his pockets and made him sit up straight in the chair.

"I hope you don't mind my asking, but will this take long?" she asked, in a voice that was altogether too saccharine. "Not that it is a problem, of course, it's just that I have an appointment this morning." She patted her hair to indicate what kind of appointment, and her smile widened even more.

She fidgeted for a moment or two sitting first this way and then the other, leaning forward resting her chin on her hand, posing as if for a photograph and staring directly into Larkin's eyes. Larkin avoided looking at her altogether and focused on his questions for the boy.

"It won't take very long, Mrs Norwell. It is just a short interview to find out what Malcolm can tell me about what happened at the flats last night."

The boy shifted in his seat as if he couldn't find a place that was comfortable. Larkin saw his mother glare at him to make him sit still and it worked, for a couple of moments, until he moved restlessly again.

"Malcolm," Larkin began.

The boy glared at him. "It's Malky."

"Malky, don't be rude. I'm sorry, he's just at that age," his mother apologised and quickly smiled again.

Larkin waited silently until Malky looked up at him. He started again. "Okay, Malky. Why don't you tell me what you remember about last night."

The boy swallowed, his eyes wandering everywhere, avoiding eye contact and then he shrugged. "Not much."

"Okay, let's start from when you met up with your friends."

"We were just hangin'. Nothing much happened."

"I was told that two of the girls, Suzie and Jenna, were fighting. Do you know why?"

He shrugged again and slumped back in his seat, staring down at his trainers. "It wasn't anything unusual. They don't get on much."

"What happened after they stopped fighting?"

"Not a lot, we just all split up after that."

"So where did you go?"

He shrugged again.

"Answer the Inspector's question, Malky."

"Can I get a drink?" He nodded at the water dispenser in the corner of the room.

Larkin got up and poured him a cup of water from the chiller. "Tell me about the fire, Malky. When did you realise the building was on fire?"

Malky shifted on his seat and took a gulp of water. "I was just messing about with a couple of mates and we heard someone shouting, so we ran round to the back of the flats, and that was when we saw the smoke."

"Which of your friends were with you when you heard the shouting?"

"Dunno." He wiped his nose on his sleeve.

"Malky!" His mother frowned at him and then she smiled apologetically at Larkin. "Now don't be silly. Surely you must remember who you were with, Malky. Was Jack with you?"

He slumped forward and reached for the spare pen that was lying on the desk, rolling it back and forward. "Naw, Jack wasn't there, he'd gone off with Suzie."

"But you weren't with them? Were you with Jenna?" Larkin asked.

He shook his head. "Naw. She was in a mood. She'd gone off with some of the other girls."

"So, who were you with?"

He stared at the desk and picked up the pen, flicking it against his fingers, faster and faster. "Just some mates," he shrugged again, "I don't remember who. Can I go now?"

"Not quite yet, Malky." Larkin decided to take a different approach. "You know where Jenna lives, don't you?"

"Yeah."

"Do you know where the fire started?"

He sifted in his seat and looked around the room before answering. "Yeah."

"Where was that?"

"In Jenna's flat."

"Who told you that?"

"Jenna, she was right upset about it."

"Does that surprise you?"

He shrugged.

"So, you weren't with Jenna last night when she discovered the flats were on fire?"

"We were round at the back of the flats, when Jenna and her pals came running and she was screaming, getting hysterical, like."

"Does that surprise you? Her family could have been in the

flat."

"Naw, they were all away at some family party, so there was no one at home." He looked up quickly.

"Did Jenna tell you all her family were out that night?"

"Yeah. Yeah, everyone knew." He swallowed and wiped his nose on his sleeve again. "Jenna had been going on about it for ages saying she didn't want to go but they were making her go because everyone, all the family, had to be there for some reason."

"Do you think anyone had problems with Jenna or her family, because they are Asian?"

"Dunno."

"Did it bother you?"

He started fiddling with the pen again as he shook his head. "Naw, Jenna's pretty cool and no one bothers her, especially with those cousins of hers. No one messes with them."

"Have you had problems with her cousins, Malky?"

"Naw! I told you. No one messes with them."

DON'T JUDGE ME
Malky

I wasn't looking forward to going to the police station and Mum had been going mental all morning, getting all dressed up, like. You'd think we were going to see the Queen or something. I didn't want to go but Mum said I had to. In the end it wasn't anything like it is on the TV. There was no point in my going anyway, I mean, I wasn't about to tell them anything, was I?

I really like Jenna.

Her straight hair is so black and silky, her skin so smooth and it always looks like she has a great tan. She smells like — I don't know, just really good. I can't believe that she wanted to go out with me, Me? I still look at myself in the mirror of a morning and wonder how I got to be this good looking, but lucky, yeah, I'm the luckiest guy alive.

Then there's 'Mad Chick' Suzie. She's pretty hot when she's not plastered and I think she fancies me, too. Boy, I am hot, so hot I'm on fire! But I have to watch it because Jenna hates Suzie so I have to pretend I don't like it when Suzie comes over and starts on at me, trying to make out we have something going on. Jenna always loses her rag at that. But Suzie and me go back years, and there's nothing between us, really. She's a bit too crazy for me.

Jenna is sweet on me and that kind of makes up for the way her parents treat me. Her old man hates the idea that his daughter might be soiled by going out with a white boy like me. He probably wouldn't mind if I was minted, some chance.

He has no idea that Jenna and I have been going with each other for months. Jenna says we have to keep it quiet or her cousins will come for me and she looks really scared when she says it.

I told her I could take them, but she looked terrified and shook her head, "No, you don't, Malky, they are real trouble. We have to keep it quiet. Just between us."

She hates her parents because they are going to try and make her marry some old dude from India or Pakistan, or somewhere. So I had an ace idea about how to make it all right for Jenna and me. It took a bit of planning but...

CHAPTER 10

Gran woke from her nap and thought it was surprisingly dark. She was confused. How long had she been asleep? It hadn't been dark when she'd dozed off, had it? She felt a tickle in her throat that turned into a cough. The air, as she drew in a breath, was hot and burning.

It wasn't dark outside. The room had filled with choking black smoke. She couldn't stop coughing and that made her breathe in more which made her cough and retch until she could hardly stop. Her throat hurt and her eyes were streaming and stinging; she couldn't see and she couldn't breathe. The heat was becoming unbearable. She knew she had to get out of the house but her old joints were stiff. She cursed herself for choosing this particular chair because it was very soft and low. She should have sat in the other one, her favourite, but it was much too upright when she was tired, so she had settled into the comfy one to have a quick nap before she went to her Bingo.

She could hardly breathe now and coughing was draining all her energy. She wondered for a brief moment if it was worth the effort of getting up when it would probably all be over for her very soon, anyway.

*****

The first fireman into the house found the old lady collapsed in the hallway, just a few feet from the front door. There was no time to check if she was alive so he lifted her limp, frail body easily and carried her out into the fresh air where the ambulance crew were waiting.

He ran back inside to check the other rooms. No one was

sure how many people were in the house, but the next few minutes were critical; there was only a slight chance of finding anyone alive unless they were found quickly. The fire had taken hold and thick oily smoke filled each room from floor to ceiling. If the old lady had survived it would be because she had fallen onto the floor where the smoke was thinner and there was still a little air.

*****

Jack heard his phone's ringtone, the Star Wars theme, as he walked back home from Suzie's house with his mother. They had been walking in a heavy silence, neither of them keen to start the conversation that was bound to end in an argument.

He was angry with her. He hated surprises and she had done her usual thing, finding out things that were none of her business, thinking she was so clever. Investigative Journalist, that's what she called herself but why didn't she just ask him instead of nosing about in his business. What possessed her to go and speak to Suzie's foster mother, stick her nose in there, too? He didn't even know she was home. It wasn't as if she had even called and told him she was back. Why couldn't she just act like a normal parent and be at home, or tell him where she was?

He wished he could go and stay with his dad but that was "not possible" she told him. He'd tried calling his dad but his new wife answered the phone and said she would take a message. His dad never called him back and when he told his mother she just made a face and said "Typical!"

What kind of answer was that?

He glanced at the screen on his phone before answering it. It was Malky.

"Jack!" Malky's voice roared out of the phone, above a background of sirens. Jack realised he wasn't only hearing the sirens down the phone, they were close by. There was a strange smell in the air, but he was only aware of it subliminally. He would remember the smell later.

"Malky? What's up? Where are..."

"Jack!" Malky didn't let him finish. "Where are you? You've gotta get home — *right now.*"

"I'm almost there. What's going o..." Jack turned the corner and stopped, the words half formed. The scene before him was unbelievable and it took a few moments to make any sense of it at all. There were four fire engines, two ambulances and crowds of people — and they were all gathered outside his house.

Two steady streams of water fountained into the air from fire hoses, splattering onto the house. Thick plumes of black smoke rose from a hole in the roof just above his bedroom window.

Malky ran up to Jack and grabbed his arm, propelling him towards one of the ambulances. "It's your Gran, Jack. She was in the house, they've just brought her out."

Jack felt as if he'd been thumped in the chest. Gran?

He was vaguely aware of the sound of his mother wailing, "Mum? Oh no, Mum! Is she ...? Oh no!"

One of the green-suited paramedics took his mother to one side and spoke to her for a moment before escorting her into the ambulance while Jack stood staring at the circus of emergency vehicles surrounding his house. Smoke billowed from every window and he saw a lick of flame appear, to be swiftly extinguished by a shoot of water from one of the fire hoses.

Malky was speaking to him but Jack only heard a mumbling

noise and the roaring in his head. Nothing made sense. It couldn't have been... No!

Anyway, why was Gran even in the house, she was supposed to be at the Bingo. This was Bingo day. She never missed it, ever. Maybe someone had made a mistake, perhaps it wasn't her, and his mother would come out in a moment and tell him it was all a mistake. But he knew he was hanging on a flimsy thread of hope.

"You'll have to move back, lads."

Jack stared at the policeman as if he was some alien speaking a foreign language. A jumble of thoughts tumbled about in his head and made no sense. Something buzzed near to the surface of his mind but it was as if he was looking at words in his head yet couldn't read them.

"It's his house," Malky told the policeman.

Jack's thoughts fell into place with an imperceptible thud. He didn't want to believe it could be true, it wasn't possible, was it? But he knew it was. He knew exactly what had happened.

His mother stepped down from the ambulance and came over to them. She was pale and looked shaken.

Jack moved past her towards the open doors. "I want to see Gran! I didn't mean... I didn't know..." Thoughts spinning in his head. "Is she going to be okay?"

"Gran's still alive. She's inhaled a lot of smoke. They're worried she might develop pneumonia because of all the smoke in her lungs."

He was aware of his mother's voice sounding uncharacteristically high, almost hysterical as she stood behind him, her hand on his shoulder. But Jack could only stare at the small figure on the stretcher. It hardly looked like Gran. Her face was covered with an oxygen mask and her normally neat silver hair was darkened with soot. There were dark sooty smudges on the wrinkles of her hands, her soft, kind hands.

Gran, who never wished anything bad on anyone.

He felt sick and he only got as far as the bushes beside the ambulance before he lost his lunch. His head was thumping. But how could it have happened, it was too long ago, wasn't it? This wasn't meant to happen. Why had Gran been in the house, she went to Bingo the same time every single week. She never missed her Bingo, not ever. She shouldn't even have been there at all.

CHAPTER 11

DI Larkin helped himself to another biscuit from the plate. He didn't really like ginger creams but he needed the sugar. This case was becoming more complicated by the minute and the Superintendent was breathing down his neck to get answers. Each time he thought he'd got somewhere, something else turned up that changed everything again.

"Look at the facts," he remembered his old friend and mentor telling him when he was a rookie on his first case. "When everything is becoming clouded with emotion or personalities, let the facts talk for themselves. But don't ignore your gut instincts completely, especially when you've been in the job for a while."

What were the facts?

There had been two fires.

Was there one arsonist, or two? Could either of the fires be accidental?

The report on how the first fire started in the flats was to arrive on his desk today but he was fairly sure it would confirm what they suspected. The initial report had suggested it was accelerator on rags pushed through the letterbox but made worse by inflammable material behind the door.

But who, and why?

There were several possibilities and the only witness... Why was nothing ever simple?

He took another bite of the biscuit, wincing as it lodged itself in his tooth, sending a shaft of pain into his skull. He needed to get to the dentist, but he couldn't spare the time just now. He swallowed down a swig of hot coffee, which just made it worse.

Why? That was the next question. Racism was the easy

conclusion to jump to. The family seemed to be well liked in the community, but that didn't mean there wasn't someone with a grudge against them. The girl, Suzie, was clearly in the frame, she wasn't a friend of Jenna Chowdhury, but although Suzie had a history of trouble a mile long, for some reason he really didn't think she had done it, but he couldn't say why, exactly. His gut instinct working again?

All the kids seemed jittery and it felt like more than just because they were being called in for interviews. The boy, Jack, was by all accounts a popular lad, and Malky struck Larkin as a follower, rather than an instigator.

There was a knock at the door.

"Come in."

"Are you ready, Sir? I have Mrs Sorley, Jack's mother, here to see you."

"Right, Tom, send her in."

The woman came in surrounded by a cloud of expensive perfume. She was dressed in what Larkin imagined were high-priced designer clothes, not that he knew much about that kind of thing.

"Please sit down, Mrs Sorley. I am Detective Inspector Larkin."

"Hello." Self-assured and confident, she reached out to shake his hand. Her nails were long and perfectly manicured in a deep crimson that matched her scarf and handbag. Her voice was deceivingly soft but the look in her eyes said that this woman was no pushover.

With a brief glance she inspected the seat at her side of the desk. Larkin almost expected her to dust it off but she just smiled at him and sat down, elegantly crossing her legs and sitting forward. Despite the makeup and smart clothes he could see her eyes looked strained and tired, and her smile had a hard edge to it.

"How is your mother?" Larkin asked.

"She is a little better, thank you for asking. The smoke inhalation has caused her some breathing problems but they expect her to make a full recovery."

"We don't have the fire report yet, but do you have any idea what might have caused the blaze?"

She shook her head. "I've been away for the last month. In New York, covering a story for my paper," she added quickly. "I have to work. Jack's father is... Anyway, I had just got back and my mother told me that my son had been questioned about that other fire. I went off straight away to try and find him.

'We were returning to the house when we saw the fire engines. It was horrible. I could hardly believe it when they said my mother had been in the house and they'd had to rescue her from the blaze. I still can't believe it. She normally goes out to meet her friends in the afternoon, although she did tell me at lunch time that she was feeling a little tired, so she must have decided to stay at home."

"Does your mother smoke, Mrs Sorley?"

"Never!" She gave him a look that could have cut through him. "Disgusting habit."

"Does Jack?"

"No! No one in the family ever has! Jack was very ill as a child and he had asthma so we were always very careful about not having any smokers in the house."

Larkin smiled to ease the tension. "I just needed to check."

"Do you know what caused the fire, Detective?"

"We're still waiting for the report. But can you tell me a bit about Jack."

"What do you want to know about him? I was led to believe you have already interviewed him."

"Yes, I did. Your mother brought him in yesterday. But I am just trying to get some background information, to understand him a little better. What kind of boy is he?"

She shrugged. "I don't know what you mean. He's just a normal boy. Bright, of course."

Larkin tapped his pen on the desk while he thought how he could ask the question. "Has he... been in trouble. At school for instance?"

"I don't know what you're getting at, Detective. Jack is a bright, intelligent boy, almost top of his class. And no, he's never been in trouble."

"Has Jack said anything about Tuesday night?"

Her perfectly shaped eyebrows drew down into a scowl. "Detective Larkin, you do realise that my mother, Jack's grandmother, nearly died in that fire? So, no, he's not said much about Tuesday night. It's got nothing to do with Jack and we've had more important things on our minds!"

Larkin took a deep breath. "Of course, I'm sorry. I know you must be concerned about your mother, but," he held up his hand to halt any further complaint, "there is something else you should know. We have a witness who puts Jack at the scene of the fire on Tuesday."

She sat for a moment, her expression carefully controlled to reveal nothing. "I don't know what you are insinuating. As far as I know Jack was at the scene of the fire, but so were a lot of others. There is no reason to imagine he had anything to do with it."

She shrugged off the possibility, getting to her feet. "It's plainly ridiculous and I won't have you insinuating things about my son!"

CHAPTER 12

Jenna's father had dropped her off at the door of her aunt's house when they returned from the police station. She slung her jacket over the hook in the hallway and wandered into the large kitchen where her mother was cooking. Her mother loved to cook. Jenna drew in the familiar smells and they were oddly reassuring. In the midst of all the chaos it made her feel as if some things at least might still be a little like normal.

"What did the policeman say, Jenna?" her mother asked. She stopped stirring the pot to add some spices from a dish beside her.

"Not much, I don't know if they have any idea who did it yet. Where's Aunt Mela?" Jenna was hoping her aunt was out.

"She has gone to speak to Pavan's parents today. Your aunt has worked hard to organise this for you. I know you are not sure about him but he seems like a good man and it is a good match."

"Why does she have to interfere? I can't stand him! He makes my skin crawl. Why can't you let me choose the person I want to marry? I know you and dad had an arranged marriage, but what about cousin Sara. We never hear from her and you know she is miserable. You said it yourself. How can that be a good thing?"

Her mother stared at the pot she was stirring, and said nothing.

"Why can't I live a normal life, like the rest of my friends? Why can't I choose who I want to be with?"

"Jenna, you know your father and I just want the best for you. You may not love him now but you will come to know him better, and love grows as time goes on." She turned to face her daughter. "The first time I met your father I thought he was quite ugly and a bit fat!"

Jenna smiled, she knew this story about her parents and she knew they were happy together, but that didn't mean she could ever want to live with Pavan. "I know, you've told me this before, but why won't you trust me to choose?"

"We just want you to have a good life. You are too young to make this kind of decision for yourself, to choose who is good for you and will give you what you want for your life."

"What you want for me, more like. You don't even know my friends. You've never met them!"

Silence met this remark and Jenna knew the subject was closed but she walked over and laid her head on her mother's shoulder. "How long do we have to live here?"

Putting down the spoon, her mother rested her head against Jenna's for a moment. "You know your aunt has been very kind to let us all stay here, Jenna. We should be grateful to her. She does a lot to help us, and to help your father, too."

"I know," she muttered. "I just think she's a bully. She keeps telling you and father what to do."

"You shouldn't say such things, Jenna. She's just trying to advise and help us. She is very kind at heart. She has helped us a lot, you know."

"I suppose so, but..."

The front door opened and like a tornado her aunt swept into the kitchen. She never entered a room quietly. "I've just been to see Pavan's parents and they are prepared to forgive Jenna for her rudeness, especially as they feel sorry for you with the situation you all find yourselves in now." She sank into a comfortable chair and sighed as if she was exhausted. "At least that is good. If they are making excuses for you it means they haven't decided to forget the whole thing."

Jenna had to bite her tongue. Her mother would not be

pleased if she was rude to her aunt but there was no need for the woman to be quite so patronising.

"I told them how I had offered you my house to use as your own since yours has been destroyed and they appreciated how I need to put my family first, whatever the personal cost." She glared at Jenna, with her small piercing eyes. "They understand duty and responsibility to family!"

Jenna opened her mouth, but before she could speak her mother interrupted.

"Jenna." Her mother spoke in a quiet tone as she always did, such a contrast to her aunt's loud and penetrating voice. "I am almost finished here, so perhaps you might go upstairs and get yourself ready so that we can go out, as we discussed, to get you some clothes to replace those that were lost in the fire."

Jenna nodded, not trusting herself to speak. She knew her mother wanted to stop her answering her aunt back and causing an argument. She was tempted to do it anyway except that it would cause her mother distress, and her mother's eyes were still red from crying.

CHAPTER 13

At first Malky had tried to scribble the note with his left hand so that no one would know it was him but he realised quite quickly that it wasn't going to work. He picked up the scissors and scanned the newspaper for another word. There it was. He almost had the whole thing now. At first he didn't know what to do, but then he saw an article about arranged marriages and some group that was protesting about them. That was what had given him the idea.

It was taking forever trying to find the words he needed in the headlines, and to cut them up while he was wearing his gloves. He felt a bit like a secret agent, trying to make sure he left no fingerprints and things like that. But no one ever told you how difficult and boring it was trying to find the words you needed in newspapers or how difficult it was to handle scissors with gloves on.

He realised that in films they always used those thin gloves that you see doctors and nurses wear but he didn't have any so he was wearing his winter knitted gloves, but they were a bit thick and it was awkward.

He'd got hold of a load of newspapers from their neighbour's house. They had all been wrapped together ready to go out for recycling. Malky smiled to himself. He was recycling them, wasn't he?

Now he had it all done and he carefully laid the words out in the right order and read it through.

ARRANGED **MARRIAGES** are **WRONG.**

The **FIRE was A** *warning*

Yes, that would work, he knew it would!

He glued them onto the sheet and as soon as the glue had dried he folded it up and stuffed it into his pocket. He had to put it somewhere Jenna's parents would find it but he had to make sure no one saw him leave it. He'd do it during the night when no one would be around.

*****

It was almost midnight before he was sure his mum had gone to sleep. He'd crept out of his room twice earlier in the night, only to discover her light was still on. Slipping downstairs, he grabbed his jacket from the newel post at the foot of the stairs, carefully avoiding the last step that always creaked with a groan like a wounded soldier.

The streets were silent, and his footsteps echoed on the damp pavement in tandem with his rapid heartbeat. It wasn't far to Jenna's aunt's house and as he crossed the road he could see that all the houses were in darkness; that was good. He'd remembered to bring his gloves and slipped them on before taking the paper out of his pocket and smoothing it out between his fingers and thumbs.

The late night bus came around the corner at the far end of the street, its bright interior lighting up the pavement. He held his breath.

Please let it keep on going. Don't stop!

He didn't want anyone to see him going to the house. What if her cousins were on the bus? What if they caught him? He always told Jenna that they didn't bother him, that he wasn't scared of them, but that was just bravado. They terrified him. He didn't want to think what they would do if they caught him near their house. He stuffed the sheet of paper back into his pocket.

Malky felt his heartbeat start to gallop and he shrunk into his jacket and turned his face towards the side of the hood, watching out of the corner of his eye. He was now walking very slowly; his feet seemed reluctant to go any closer.

Please don't stop. Don't let it be the cousins.

The bus slowed slightly and he could see two figures standing up, ready to get off. Malky felt his insides melting and his stomach churning. His leg muscles were like mush, hardly able to hold him up.

He realised he had stopped walking and forced himself to take another step, to try and look as if he was just walking down the road, minding his own business. He could run the other way but he was too scared to think straight and had to keep going forwards.

The bus drew into the side of the road at the bus stop. The doors swept open discharging the passengers, who stepped down and started walking towards him.

Malky was still a few houses away from Jenna's aunt's house and he walked as slowly as he could, breathing fast, his arms tight at his sides and hands jammed down into his pockets for security.

He could see that the two men were tall and heavily built. As they approached the path leading to Jenna's aunt's house one stopped, suddenly, and the other looked straight at Malky.

He thought his heart would explode. It was thundering in his ears as his eyes flickered around looking for an escape route, but there was a tall hedge running all along the street beside him and aside from turning to go back the way he had come, there was nowhere else to go.

With a tiny flash of light, the man who had stopped lit a cigarette. A moment later they both started walking again, coming towards him. They were talking to each other and didn't seem to be taking much notice of him, but Malky thought this could be a ploy to lull him into a false sense of security. He could hardly bear to keep walking but he had to, and now they were almost in front of him. He put his head down and partially hid his face in his hood and away from them, grinding his teeth together.

He could feel his arms shaking as they passed him on the pavement, waiting for them to stop to grab him or to say something, but the two men just walked past. Malky gasped in a long breath that tasted sweet with relief. He glanced behind him and watched as they continued along the road, walking away from him.

He was almost at Jenna's aunt's house now. He grabbed the sheet from his pocket and once again smoothed out the crumpled edges. Checking that the two men had gone and there was no one watching, he ran quickly down the path and pushed it through the letterbox.

CHAPTER 14

Suzie followed Jack as they went in through the back door of his house. The policeman had lifted the yellow tape to allow them into the burnt out hallway.

"You've got five minutes," the policeman told them. "But I doubt you'll find anything. Almost everything has either been destroyed by the fire or taken by the forensics people. Don't go upstairs, it's not safe."

The house smelled terrible, a burnt choking smell that caught in the back of her throat. The air was laden with damp soot and the floor was covered in bits of soggy paper, and shattered ornaments.

"At least you've got a family," Suzie said, continuing their conversation. She couldn't understand what Jack had to be so angry about. He had no idea. "And they don't, they aren't..."

She turned away from him and kicked at the blackened edge of a cupboard but it crumbled into ashes, coating her boots. "You have your Gran, too. She cares about you. Don't ever wish for a brother, they're not worth having. They don't care."

Jack turned to her, a frown on his face. "A brother? You never said you had a brother."

"I don't! Not any more," she growled and walked through to the back bedroom.

It had been Gran's room. The windows, streaked with soot, let in very little light and the walls were black and damp to the touch. Jack tried to remember what the wallpaper had looked like but he couldn't see past the dark smoke-stained walls. The carpet was burnt and squelched underfoot where it had been soaked by the water used to put out the fire. There wasn't much of anything left.

The fireman had told them that the fire had started in his mother's bedroom just along the hall, but between the fire, smoke and the water used to put it out, most of the house had been destroyed.

Jack followed Suzie into the living room and came up behind her, pulling her back towards him, not sure if he was comforting her or the other way around, he just knew it felt right.

"But you did have a family once, didn't you?"

"It wasn't a family. Dad, and the step-witch he married, only wanted us kids to use us. No one cared what happened to us." Her voice became quiet and he could hardly make out the words.

"What happened to your mother?"

"I can't remember much about her." Suzie hesitated. "She smelt like flowers, I think. I don't really remember. Sy used to tell me she'd gone to live with the angels and I could picture her with long golden hair and wings. Silly, isn't it. She died when I was really small. It might have been when my baby sister, Leila, was born or soon after but I don't know anything else about her.

'Used to miss Sy a lot but it's been so long I probably wouldn't know him if I did see him. Sy used to try to make sure Leila and I didn't get beaten up by all the weirdos that came into the house for drugs... and things. But he couldn't be there all the time and I sometimes heard him shouting at dad and the step-witch, before they sent him off places, to get him out of the house. He would leave, and then the doorbell went..."

Jack felt her whole body shaking as she spoke. He held her closer.

"I remember Leila crying a lot. She never smiled, and she couldn't sleep, except when I sang to her. No one cared what happened to us until eventually the Social came and took us away. By then it was already too late, we were broken. Leila was just four then and I never saw her again."

Suzie pulled herself out of his arms and stood staring at the soot-covered window.

"I tried to tell them she wouldn't sleep unless I was there to hold her and sing to her, but they wouldn't listen. I don't know where they took her. I kept asking and trying to find her but no one would tell me where she was." She wiped her eyes with the back of her hand, leaving a smear of black ash across her cheek.

"Sy said he would come back for me but he never did. I used to wait by the windows in the children's home, waiting for him to come but eventually I realised it was a waste of time. He was never going to come for me."

Jack wiped away the dark smudge on her cheek with his thumb. "Maybe he doesn't know where you are?"

"No." She shook her head and turned away from him. "Don't want to talk about it. Can we go? There's nothing here, is there?" Jack suddenly had to get out of the house. He wasn't sure why he had insisted they come. It had seemed a good idea at the time. He'd thought he needed to see it, but now he was here he just felt sick. "No, let's get out of here."

CHAPTER 15

Jenna stepped into her aunt's house, quietly closing the door behind her. She didn't feel like speaking to anyone, especially her nosy and opinionated aunt.

She crossed the hallway and, hearing voices in the lounge, she stopped to listen for a moment before going in.

Her mother and her aunt were speaking and she heard her name. Drawing closer to the gap in the door she could hear her aunt's voice, a nasal sound that made everything she said sound like a complaint. She was talking about the party.

"You know, sister, Pavan's family is a good catch for your Jenna. She needs to show them she is interested, before they change their minds. I'm not saying it's your fault she behaved badly, but... well, with these young girls not always behaving as they should... It becomes a disgrace to the whole family... and it can't be allowed to continue."

Jenna scowled. Her Aunt Mela was always criticising her, and trying to make out she was better than Jenna's mother because Aunt Mela had three sons and Jenna was an only child, worse still she was a mere girl. "Pavan's family thought she was beautiful, his mother told me so herself." Her mother's voice was gentle and coaxing, almost pleading. Jenna wished her mother was more forceful and didn't always give in to her aunt about everything.

"Of course, Dharma, Jenna is beautiful, but they will want to know she is obedient, too. It was quite rude to Pavan and his parents, her leaving the party like that to go off and meet up with boys. It brings dishonour on all of us."

Jenna hoped the noise of her grinding teeth wouldn't travel into the room beyond. Her aunt was so patronising. Her beloved sons were thugs but they could do anything they liked and no one bothered. Her mother's next words shocked Jenna to the core.

"No, sister, I don't think she was rude at all, she wasn't feeling well."

Her aunt snorted. "She was well enough to go out with her friends."

"We don't want to break her heart." Her mother's voice was so soft that Jenna almost didn't catch her next words. "She is so precious to us. We would never force her into anything she really didn't want."

Jenna could hardly believe it. That was not what her mother had said to her. Could it be true?

"Well, she's your child. Perhaps she will not let you down. I do think you are too soft on her, Dharma. But you mustn't worry about it just now; you have had a terrible shock. I'm sure it won't be a problem and it will all turn out well." Jenna heard the lie in her aunt's voice. "I have asked Hasan to speak to your husband and I am sure they will find a way to work this all out."

Jenna felt her face flush as she listened. Her aunt and her cousin were going to put pressure on her father.

They had no right.

She stepped quietly away from the door and silently climbed the stairs. Throwing herself on her bed, she wanted to scream but she didn't want anyone to hear so she beat at the pillow, tears streaming down her face. What was she to do now? She felt so guilty, but equally she was angry that her aunt and her cousins were sticking their noses into her life. She knew her parents listened to what they said. They would feel pressured into making her marry Pavan. She shuddered at the thought of him touching her, kissing her. It made her feel sick.

Her life was in ruins.

The bag of clothes she had left behind the caretaker's cupboard in the flat's stairwell had been destroyed with everything else. She'd thought there would be time to go back and collect it when she had told Malky about what was happening at home and how she had to get away. She'd had all these plans about how they could take a train and live together in a big city, where no one knew them. She'd even taken some money that her mum had hidden away in a secret stash and because of the fire her mum didn't even know it was gone.

Normally she would never have touched it, her parents let her have an allowance and they were quite generous. But she had needed more than what was left in her savings account and anyway she couldn't get at that immediately. She needed some cash to use right away, to make sure they could stay somewhere clean when they got to the city. She couldn't bear ending up in some sleazy bedsit.

It would have been fine, but she hadn't expected to fall out with Malky. In her imagination she had thought they could run away together and it would all be great. That was before she got there and found him with Suzie all over him on the street corner. She had been so angry with him, with her parents and everything. It was all horrible. Her life was rubbish. No one cared what she wanted, no one cared about her, even Malky couldn't be trusted. She hated them all.

Her father always said she had a terrible temper but her parents had insisted that she learn to control it and she did, normally, but that didn't stop her feeling ready to tear things apart.

The night of the fire, when she met Pavan, she had felt like a raging goddess, angry with everyone and hungry to take it out on those around her. Now she didn't know what she felt. The money she had taken was like molten metal in her pocket, telling her that taking it had been wrong, that she should give it back to her mother. But that would raise all sorts of questions about why she'd taken it in the first place.

If it wasn't that the police were already involved and might come looking for her, she might have thought about leaving home right now. But on her own? That had never been the plan. Not that it had been much of a plan, she saw that now. It had been wrecked by Malky that night, and even today he seemed strange, distant and saying all the wrong things. Things that showed he didn't really understand her at all. Did he even love her? She wasn't sure now. Some of the things he said... And he was so sullen, not aware of how upset and shaken she was by it all. Everything was in ruins.

Her pillow was damp already but the tears just didn't seem to stop. She was lost, lonely and alone. She slipped into her dreams and she was suddenly right back there. It was the night of the fire.

*****

A little out of breath and furious that it was so late, Jenna fumbled with her keys looking for the right one for her front door, but the more she tried to hurry the more they slipped through her fingers.

"This is silly," she told herself, stopping for a moment to take a deep breath and look properly at the bunch of keys in her hand. She untangled the long twisted chain of her favourite keyring, a birthday present from Malky. It had her initials strung out along the chain and there was a little dog at the end of it. But it kept on getting snared up with everything else.

She opened the door and dropped her bags and her coat,

shrugging out of her clothes as she made her way to her room. She didn't want to take any longer than she had to, she was late already and she had to put her plan into action. She pulled on her tight jeans and cropped top, changed her earrings and started to comb her hair. Her make-up would need to be redone, too.

As she reapplied her mascara Jenna thought about what she would pack. She would need enough clothes, but not so many that her bag would be too heavy to carry. She had to get some money; she had some savings but not enough to keep her going for long and she didn't know how long they would have to last her.

Finally, make-up done, she kneeled on the carpet and pulled her favourite pink bag out from under the bed. It would be just the right size.

For the next few minutes she was entirely focussed on packing, several things were put in and taken out again as she changed her mind or they took up too much space. Eventually the bag was full. She would have to make do with what she had and when she got a job she could buy some new clothes.

She felt a buzz of excitement. She could imagine being away with Malky, just the two of them, doing what they wanted and in charge of their own lives.

She still needed some more money. Her mother kept a jar of cash that she said she was saving for a rainy day. Well, this was Jenna's rainy day, at least it certainly felt like it and she deserved it, didn't she, after putting up with this evening.

In the cupboard in her parent's bedroom she reached up to the top shelf and brought down the jar. She took it all and then just as she was about to close it and put it back, she stopped. An empty jar would look suspicious, so she peeled off a couple of notes and put them back. Before she could feel too guilty, she reached up to replace the jar, dislodging a piece of paper on the shelf. It fluttered to the floor.

As Jenna picked it up her eye caught some of the wording.

"No way!"

It was a photocopy of a letter from her father to her aunt giving her aunt ownership of their flat, their home, as security for a loan. It was dated just six months before and it was due to be repaid next week. Jenna knew her father had been really worried about something but her parents never talked to her about things like that.

Like a tumbling dice several things fell into place. Things she had not really thought about. But little details all became clear now that she knew about the loan. This was why her aunt was able to bully them all so much. She had organised this marriage because if her niece, Jenna, married into Pavan's family it would be great for her aunt's business. It was nothing to do with her parents, it was all about her aunt.

If she left home her parents wouldn't have to worry because there would be no marriage for her aunt to hold over them. There was also the matter of the loan. Well, perhaps she could do something about that. But did she dare? She stuffed the paper into her bag.

It all seemed perfect. Jenna smiled to herself as she tucked a few notes in her pocket and pushed the rest of the wad of notes deep inside the bag and zipped it closed.

Looking around her room she felt a tinge of sadness. She loved her parents and she would miss her room and all her things but she knew she had to do it. She had to go otherwise they would make her marry Pavan and all the rest of her life would be planned out by him and his parents. They were just as controlling as her aunt.

She picked her jacket off the hook behind the door and collected her keys from the floor where she had dropped them when she'd come home.

She had just one more thing to do before she left.

A few minutes later, carefully closing the front door behind her, Jenna was too busy with her own thoughts to notice the two figures walking down the path to the flats.

When she turned around and saw them a flash of fear travelled across her body. It was her cousins. What were they doing here?

Her aunt's side of the family were very conservative and her cousins were always complaining that she was not behaving well. They had already warned her about being seen with Malky. Jenna was a little scared of them, of what they might do, and she didn't want them asking her questions about what she had in the bag.

She tossed the bag behind the caretaker's cupboard close to the doorway and stepped away from it as quickly as she could so that she met them just outside the flats.

"Jenna? What are you doing here?" Hasan was the older of the two and the one Jenna was most scared of. Her mother had warned her not to get on the wrong side of him. He and his brother exchanged looks but Hasan was the one who made all the decisions.

She took a deep breath and glared back at him "Could ask you the same question, Hasan."

He towered over her, threatening. It was what he did best, Jenna thought.

"Why are you not with your parents? You were to be meeting with Pavan's family, tonight. You'd better not do anything to sour that arrangement."

She knew her face was flushed. "I... I wasn't ... I..."

"And what are you wearing? Have you no shame?"

Jenna instinctively pulled her jacket closed over the skimpy top.

"You are a disgrace. Your father should not let you embarrass the family like this. Does he even know where you are?"

Jenna knew she had to get away from them before he started asking any more questions. She took a deep breath and looked him in the eye.

"Yes, he does, not that it is any business of yours. Anyway, shouldn't you both be at the party? I heard your mother ask where you were."

She pushed past them and started walking away, hoping they wouldn't follow her and trying not to run however much she desperately wanted to. She could hardly believe what she had said, that she had actually stood up to him.

"You'd better not be meeting that boy, Jenna," he called after her. "I'm warning you, stay away from him or there'll be trouble."

It wasn't until she had reached the other side of the flats, and her heart had stopped trying to burst out of her chest, that she remembered her bag. She couldn't go back for it, they might still be there and see her coming. That was the last thing she wanted. She would have to come and get it later, with Malky. Would there be time? She convinced herself it would all work out. She would find Malky and they could come right back to get the bag. It was all going to be fine.

At least that was what she thought, until she saw Malky and Suzie together.

CHAPTER 16

The witness

The same policewoman — the one she had met before when she made her statement after the fire — ushered her into a small room with a tiny window in the door that was covered in a dirty, pale green Venetian blind. The string had got caught up in the spars which were twisted at one end.

She stared, fascinated by the dull stripes of light filtering through the blind, ignoring everything else around her.

The door swept open and her eyes were dragged towards the short, slightly balding man who came in. He sat down opposite her and she noticed the deep bags under his eyes. He had a kindly face, but she was still wary, glancing repeatedly at the policewoman for reassurance. She hoped the woman would stay in the room and not leave her alone with the policeman. She began to fidget with the leather handles of the handbag, clutched tightly between her and the desk.

"This is Miss Smith, Sir," the policewoman said, in a softly reassuring voice. "It's Janice, isn't it?"

She nodded, hugging her handbag closer.

"Hello, Miss Smith. I'm Detective Inspector Larkin. Do you mind if I call you Janice?" Larkin asked.

She shook her head with a quick shuddering motion not sure she could manage to answer.

The detective shuffled the papers he had placed on the desk and started to read one of them. He looked up. "You said in your statement when you came forward after the fire, that you had seen something. Would you like to tell me what exactly you saw? Just in your own words, whatever you can remember."

She looked longingly at the policewoman who just nodded

encouragingly.

"I saw them kids, a girl..." her voice dropped to a whisper as if she had run out of breath, "...and a boy. They came out of the flats. It was just before the fire. I was sitting there and they came out."

He smiled at her. "That's fine. You live on Hansley Road I think. Is that right?"

She nodded, quickly.

"That's quite far away from the flats. Can you tell me why you were there?"

"Used to... Used to... live there."

"You used to live in those flats?"

"Yes." It was a whisper.

"So did you come back to visit someone, one of your old neighbours, perhaps?" he asked.

She shook her head again and bit her lip, glancing up at the policewoman.

"Just tell DI Larkin what you told me, Janice," she said. Janice thought she had a nice smile.

Her thumbnails started digging into the leather handle of her bag, one after the other, in rapid succession. "I... I..."

The policewoman eyes widened in support, as if that would entice the words out of her mouth.

"I just wanted to go back. I wanted to see the place again. I was just sitting there when she ran out. They ran past me. I was only sitting there, minding my own business."

The policeman smiled but she knew he wanted more.

"Janice, I know this must be difficult for you but you said in your original statement that..."

Larkin paused for a moment searching for the right piece of paper. He found it and read out loud from the sheet. "The girl had a t-shirt and a leather jacket. It was short. And there was a boy. He had a hood up, it was a dark colour, but there was something on the back of his jumper." Can you tell me any more about what they looked like, these kids you saw?"

She shook her head jerkily. She didn't want to think about that night, it still scared her.

"It's very important, Janice. Can you remember what was on the back of the hoodie, perhaps?"

She pursed her lips. All she could remember was the girl, shouting at her.

*****

She sank down onto the bench, her heart thumping. She was unfit, she never ran anywhere, but she had run all the way around to the front of the block of flats to get away from them. Now she had stopped, sheltered by the trees around her. She felt a little safer, no one could creep up on her here. There was a tall wall behind the bench, and trees hiding her from anyone who might pass by.

Her hands were shaking so much that she could hardly light the cigarette. It took her three attempts before she could strike the match against the box and hold it still enough. She hated that feeling of being sick, her stomach twisted with nerves.

But those kids on the street, she could hardly bear to think about what had happened. The fighting. Their hard voices. Thinking about it conjured up the images in her mind, frightening possibilities that she had been suppressing. They were attempting to flood her mind, crashing in on her little bit of security. If they got out and she had to face them, she would be lost.

"I won't think about it. I won't!"

She pushed the thoughts and images from her mind and mentally slammed a door on them. She couldn't go there, she couldn't think about it. She had to think about something else.

The flame wavered before her eyes until it finally seared the tip of the cigarette, making it glow with a warm orange brightness. She inhaled and it glowed stronger. She drew in the smoke, feeling the pull as it flooded deep into her lungs, sharp and familiar, comforting. She knew it made her cough but she hardly noticed any more and she didn't care, why should she?

She sat still. Lifting her hand mechanically back to her mouth, she drew another lungful and then back lowered it back to the bench beside her leg. She automatically held it away from her clothes, between two stretched out fingers before she lifted it back to her mouth.

It was a full five minutes before she took notice of her surroundings again. A cool wind had struck up and there was something she had to do, something at the edge of her mind, something important. It was time.

She was about to get up when she saw someone coming out of the door to the flats. A girl, she had seen her before, but she didn't remember where. Her mind was full of her new determination and there was room for nothing else.

She watched the girl walk away. Watched her go over to the small park area beyond and link arms with a boy who was waiting for her there. She watched them turn and leave.

Grabbing her bag in her hand, she stood up. It was as if the intervening four years had never happened and she could look at the doorway with a detachment she had never felt before. Her determination was stronger than anything else. She had to do this, her counsellor had told her, before she could get better. Was it really only four years since she had lived here so happily? Before she had been left all alone in the world.

Heavy footsteps on the pavement stopped her. She withdrew again, back behind the bushes.

A boy ran up to the door, fast, his hoodie hiding his face. He looked around furtively, before disappearing into the flats. She knew he'd not seen her. He was gone in a moment, but his sudden appearance had shocked her to stillness so that he never noticed her standing there. She was used to that. She knew how to make herself almost invisible, she'd been doing it for years now.

She heard him running up the stone steps and waited to see if he would come back out again.

She would wait until that cloud covered the moon

– until she finished her cigarette

– until she was sure he was not going to come out again

– until she had counted to 60

...56,57,58...

Footsteps on the concrete stairs warned her that he was coming back down. They stopped, and she held her breath, knowing he was just inside, not far from her hiding place. She heard a small noise but the rustle of a gentle wind through the bushes behind her made it impossible to work out what it was. A moment later he burst out of the doorway and she listened to the beating of his feet, the thudding of her heart keeping time until he was gone. She took a last deep pull on the cigarette before throwing it down and twisting her foot on it, rubbing it into a mess on the ground.

As soon as she took the first steps she was committed to action, sure that this would banish the past, change things and give her back her life.

CHAPTER 17

Suzie took the scarf from her drawer and stroked out the length of it. It was so beautiful, the colours shone like jewels catching the light. There were sparkling threads all through it. That was what had drawn her to it.

Inside, deep down inside, she felt a dull darkness which she recognised and normally kept well buried. Looking at the scarf she let the feeling rise to the surface and she examined it.

It was guilt.

She knew this was Jenna's favourite scarf, a present from her grandmother before she died. Jenna had been going on for ages about having lost it.

The material was slippery, with almost a life of its own as Suzie tried to gather it together and press it down into the large envelope.

She knew what it was like to have nothing. It was sometimes the small things that you treasured, which hurt the most when they were lost. Jenna had nothing now, the fire had taken all the pretty things that Suzie had envied so much.

It was more than just that. Suzie knew what it was like to have people control your life, to force you to do things you didn't want to. She had always thought that Jenna had it easy and that her life was so perfect. Perfect parents who gave her just about anything she wanted. Jenna always had the best clothes and the latest phone. She had parents who cared about her, pretty much everything Suzie had never had. But she was beginning to realise that Jenna's life was not quite as easy as she had thought.

This morning when she'd been having breakfast there had been a story on the TV news about arranged marriages.

Normally Suzie tuned out the news because it was mostly boring but this was about 'honour killings'. An Asian man and his mother had been arrested for murdering the woman's daughter because she had refused to marry the man they had picked for her. They said she had been behaving in a way that brought dishonour to their family.

Suzie immediately thought about Jenna and how she talked about her aunt and her cousins. How she was always scared of her father finding out she and Malky were going out. How dangerous were they? It almost sounded like something out of a movie, but this was real.

The scarf was a small thing but giving it back it made her feel better about herself. How could she get it back to Jenna without her knowing who it was from?

Malky!

She would persuade him to give it to Jenna and say he'd found it in his house. The problem was that Malky wasn't particularly pleased with Suzie at the moment. He'd been really upset when she wouldn't give him the photos.

Okay, so perhaps it wasn't the best idea she'd ever had, but what did she care. It had probably been stupid to tell him about them that night, but she hadn't been able to resist. He was going on about Jenna all the time, being all pathetic. Jack hadn't arrived when he said he would and Suzie was thinking that he might not come at all. Malky kept asking what time it was and saying he thought Jenna wasn't going to get away from her family to come and meet with him.

So Suzie had told him about the photos she'd got printed. How she'd taken them on her phone the week before when he and Jenna were snogging at that party. They were pretty tame really, well, most of them, but there was one that she knew Jenna's dad would go completely mental about, if he saw it.

That was the one she'd shown Malky and when he tried to grab it she'd stuck it down her top.

For a moment she'd thought he was going to put his hand down there and grab it back but that was when Jenna had arrived and she could see him fighting with himself. Suzie smiled as she threw herself into Malky's arms, just to annoy Jenna more.

She had known he would want to get the photo back, but Suzie had also known how Jenna would have reacted if she she'd seen him with his hand down her top. She'd have gone ballistic. So he had chickened out and that was when Suzie had turned to kiss him, seeing the frustration on his face.

It had just been a joke and Suzie hadn't really thought much about it, not then. She'd been fooling about and had wanted Malky to see how Jenna was just using him. She'd had no intention of telling her parents she was going out with him.

The more she thought about doing it, the more it seemed like a good idea but now, after all that had happened, it seemed really stupid.

She realised she couldn't give the scarf to Malky, he'd probably tell Jenna she'd taken it and Jenna would get back at her for that. Suzie realised that she liked the new Jenna a bit better and didn't want things between them to go back to the way they had been before.

Turning the large envelope around in her hand, she realised that it was quite light. She could post it and it probably wouldn't cost very much. She just needed to find out what Jenna's aunt's house number was. She knew it was Marling Street and that wasn't very far away. It was annoying that she didn't know Jenna's aunt's surname otherwise she could have looked up her phone number and got the house number that way. She would have to actually go there and take a look, which would be fine as long as Jenna didn't see her.

Suzie slipped on her short black jacket and ran down the street towards town. It didn't take her long to find Marling Street and she knew she would recognise the house because Jenna had been complaining that her aunt was fanatical about her roses — how she had been incandescent when Jenna had picked one for her mother. Jenna had said she even had them growing all over the front of the house. Her aunt even had them growing all over the front of the house and Jenna hated going through the door because she always worried that a caterpillar would drop into her hair. Surely there could only be one house in the street like that.

Turning the corner it seemed that Marling Street went on forever. It was much longer than Suzie had thought and she couldn't see a house with roses on the walls, so she started walking further along.

At last she saw the house on the other side of the road. The houses on her side all had odd numbers so that meant it had to be an even number but it was still too far away to see. She kept scanning up and down the street, just in case Jenna suddenly appeared.

When she was close enough she noted that the house a few doors down from Jenna's was number 256. She stopped and counted the doors.

"It's five doors further on," she muttered to herself, "so that makes it 258, 260,262,264.... it's 266!"

Suzie turned and walked back up the way she had come, not noticing the man who got out of his car opposite number 266 and watched her for a few moments, before crossing the road towards the house.

CHAPTER 18

Larkin grimaced as he sipped his coffee, he hated it without sugar but his doctor had warned him he had to cut down. This case was growing tentacles like a voracious, deep sea octopus, and he was drowning in the detail.

Jenna's parents were obviously worried by the letter but it looked very amateurish to Larkin. Could it have been one of the kids? Malky perhaps, or Suzie? Or was this a much bigger issue? And why had Suzie been there on the street, staring at Jenna's aunt's house? Why go back if she had been the one who wrote the note?

The girl's cousins were a couple of well known thugs who got into trouble from time to time, but arson wasn't their style and why would they burn out one of their own? Racism was the other obvious card and the area had its problems but not as much as some places. It just didn't feel as if it fitted right. He was missing something. He thought the cousins might be the best bet but he had nothing on them so it was mere supposition.

He glanced at the large clock on the wall. He had about 10 minutes before his meeting with the Superintendent. He'd better get something together before that. The old man was already going mental at the way the case was erupting in full public view, just in time to spoil his chances of promotion.

He had started to make some notes last night. He opened the notepad and, raising his mug, took another taste of the bitter coffee and pushed the cup away in disgust. He had to make some sense of all this. He went back over his notes and drew a line through the things he felt were wrong.

- seemed nervous when first questioned.

?

- Got annoyed and asked if I was trying to pin it on him and Suzie - not just him, but both of them.

- Was he just being protective of Suzie or was he hiding something or trying to spread the blame?

~~[illegible] history as an arsonist or in trouble?~~

- seemed genuinely upset about the people caught in the fire.

- The second fire, Jack's Gran in hospital - ~~was that intentional?~~

- Did he start the second fire? He seemed genuinely attached to his Gran, so ~~was it the work of a double arsonist~~ or just a disgruntled teen?

- Fire started in the bedroom, possibly in a cupboard in his mother's room and Jack appears to have all sorts of issues with his mother.

- Mother seems convinced that he is a good boy, and unwilling to hear anything else but is that just to save face?

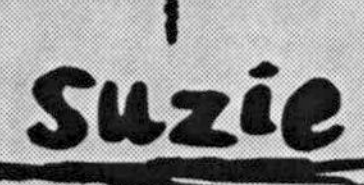

- Why was Suzie coming out of the flat of first fire, or was the witness wrong, perhaps it wasn't her?

- Why was she lurking about on Marling Street today, looking at Jenna's aunt's house? Did she write the note about arranged marriages? Seems ~~strange when she and Jenna are obviou[illegible] good friends.~~

- or is this a political issue she feels strongly about and has jumped on it as a way of getting attention?

Jenna

- Did she set first fire? Was she trying to get out of arranged marriage?
- Did she write the note herself, because she was trying to get back at parents?
- Where was she when first fire started? Still to get statements from her friends Liz and katy
- Is there something else going on with her family? Was the fire started because of something unconnected with Jenna?

Malky

- Is he bright enough to be the arsonist-
- Did he have motive for second fire? To get back at Jack for something perhaps?
- Did he write the note?
- Jenna's cousins, are they involved, seeing Malky as a threat to family name?

- How reliable was her statement?
- What did she see and what was imagined
- Get some background info on her relating to her - reliability as a witness.
- Could she have started first fire? She had previously lived in the area.
- Was it Suzie and Jack she saw or was that because they had frightened her earlier in the night and she remembered them?

Other unknown

- Arsonist- unrelated -cause of one or both fires-seems unlikely but may have been cause of first fire?

He glanced at his watch and closed the notepad, putting it in his pocket. He wasn't sure that summing it up had helped at all, he had practically nothing, but his time was up.

On his way to the Superintendent's office he stopped at the WPC's desk. "Jenny, did you get statements from the two girls that Jenna Chowdhury said she was with when the first fire started?"

"I'll get onto that right away, Sir."

"And make an appointment for Jack Sorley and his mother to come in to speak to me, as soon as possible." "Yes, sir," she said. "The Superintendent just called, he's looking for you."

Larkin forced a smile onto his face. "I'm on my way to see him now."

"Good luck, Sir!"

*****

It was well after lunchtime when he finally got away and he was starving. There was that little coffee shop that did great sandwiches and if he was lucky they might have something left, even at this time. He had almost made it out of the door when one of the uniform officers called after him.

"DI Larkin!"

Larkin turned around wearily. Was there no escape?

"There's a call for you, from forensics. There's been a development."

"I'll take it in my office," he said, heading back into the building.

He listened carefully during the call, nodding to himself. The forensics report was on its ways, the calm voice on the phone told him. Ignoring the rumble in his stomach Larkin stared at his notes.

After the way the Superintendent had been ranting at him to get the case solved, this was just what Larkin didn't need. Or perhaps it was exactly what he needed. It changed things considerably. He scratched his head and picked up his notes.

One fire had been set through the letterbox and it had destroyed the Chowdhury's ground floor flat. But there was evidence to suggest there had also been a fire started in the refuse bins below the flats, although they couldn't yet confirm what had started it. They suspected that this was what had caused the fire to take so quickly upstairs. It had channelled up through the stairwell and caused the upper flat to become filled with smoke before anyone could escape.

The same person could have done both, but not necessarily. The preliminary results suggested that the fire that had been started through the letterbox would not have caused much smoke in the stairwell for quite some time. Which suggested that the letterbox fire might have been started first.

Did this mean there had been two arsonists, weirdly setting fire to the flats at the same time, or was that too much of a coincidence? Was there just one who was taking no chances and making sure the entire place went up? That seemed much more likely.

Larkin folded his scribbled notes and stuffed them into the large pocket of his jacket. He badly needed some coffee and something to eat or his brain would refuse to work.

CHAPTER 19

Jack kicked the beer can as hard as he could and it lifted off the ground, narrowly missing the red sports car parked at the kerbside. He scuffed his heel against the ground, three, four times and picked up a stick, throwing it hard against the litterbin. But nothing was loud enough, made enough mess or damage, to soothe the grievous knot of frustration in his stomach.

He'd done it.

He'd done it, no one else.

That he'd not meant it to go that far didn't make any difference. He was the one who'd done it. He couldn't take things back or make them un-happen.

They said it was the shock, that her lungs were unable to cope with the smoke and that had led to the pneumonia. It didn't matter what they said because he knew he'd done it. And however often he'd been annoyed or irritated with her, he hadn't meant it. He had never wanted anything to happen to her.

His mother said he had to go there this morning and he had to dress up smartly, as if that made any difference. She wouldn't bother, Gran never did.

His mother was all weepy and pathetic, but it was all her fault. It was always all her fault, but she never saw that, did she?

He kicked the litterbin, once, twice. It made a small dent in the shiny black surface. He had to do something. The dark ball of anger inside was exploding and needed a channel. He was getting ready to do it again when he heard someone behind him, shouting his name. He knew it was Malky but he didn't want to speak to anyone, so he took off, slapping his feet hard against the pavement. He didn't care where he was going, he just wanted to keep on running.

The rain started and in a few moments it was pouring. He felt the water dripping down his neck and plastering his hair to his face. When he finally walked through the door of the B&B, his clothes and hair were soaking wet.

"Where have you been?" His mother's voice was a quiet shriek, but no less full of anger. She never made a spectacle of herself, ever. One of the things he hated about her was that eternal control, worrying what others might think. He didn't care what they thought, and today neither should she. She wasn't the one who mattered, it was Gran, but she never saw that, did she?

His mother was standing in the hallway with both hands splayed out flat in front of her slowly pushing down an imaginary weight. He wondered if she realised how stupid that looked.

Taking a deep breath before she spoke, her voice was controlled into its hard, normal tone. "Never mind that now." She took another deep breath to steady herself. "I'll have words with you later. Now get up those stairs and change into the clothes I've laid out for you. You'd better get down here again in the next five minutes or I'll come up and get you."

He squelched up the stairs and into the bedroom. He stood for a few moments looking at the clothes on the bed — a new pair of black trousers, a blue and white shirt and beside them a new tie, still in a cellophane cover. This was his mother's idea of 'smart' clothes and they would make him look a right prat but he didn't care any more.

He peeled off his wet jeans and hoodie and left them in a heap in the middle of the floor. It wasn't long before he was back downstairs. His wet trainers had made the clean socks damp already and he was uncomfortable but he didn't really care, he had zoned out. He didn't want to go and she would never understand that, but he had no choice.

The hospital was in the middle of town and his mother was determined to find a parking place closer than the main shopper's car park, so that she didn't have to walk far in her high heels. But she struggled to find a gap and was getting more and more irritated until in the end she was forced to head back to the multi-storey car park.

As they walked through the Mall to get to the main street, he saw Malky and Jenna walking towards them, with Suzie following just behind. Jack wondered why they were all there but he didn't want to speak to them. He didn't want to speak to anyone. It was all too complicated, all too confusing. Nothing made sense anymore.

"Isn't that Malcolm and Suzie, Jack?" his mother asked.

Suzie had sent him several text messages but he'd not responded to any of them. He knew she wanted to speak to him.

Now they had spotted him and he wasn't going to be able to avoid them. He could already see Malky staring at his clothes and wearing a stupid grin. The last thing he needed was Malky and his stupid comments.

"We're going to be late, Mum."

"You've got time to say hello."

Jack wondered why she'd suddenly become so concerned about him speaking to his friends?

"Hi Jack." Malky's grin got bigger and Jack felt like thumping him. "What you doin'? Nice gear," he smirked.

Jack looked away. He was trying to avoid eye contact with Suzie, too. Why couldn't everyone leave him alone?

"Jack?" He knew his mother was staring at him, her eyes

boring into the back of his skull. He flushed. She was treating him as if he was five years old. "We're off to visit Jack's Gran in the hospital," she told them when it became obvious that he wasn't going to speak to them at all.

"We're off to Joe's. D'you want to meet us there afterwards?" Suzie asked, trying to move around Malky and catch Jack's eye.

When he avoided her and started walking away, his mother answered for him. "We won't be very long, visiting time is just from 2-4pm today. I'm sure Jack will meet you there after that."

He could hear her high heeled shoes clatter as she tried to catch up with him but he didn't slow down. He walked out of the Mall without looking back and turned right towards the hospital.

By the time his mother finally caught up with him he had reached the hospital doors. They walked in silence to the lift and waited for it to arrive. He could feel her silent anger and something inside him wanted to cheer. It was a short ride in the lift but he would have been happy if it had gone on forever, he wanted to be anywhere else but here.

CHAPTER 20

Suzie watched Jack walking away from them. She didn't know what to do. "Has he said anything to you, Malky? I can't get him to speak to me."

Malky shook his head. "Nah, won't answer his phone, or anything. I saw him this morning on the street, but when I called he just ignored me and ran off."

"He's upset about his Gran." Suzie fished about in her pocket for her phone. "He's really close to her, isn't he? After all he lives with her most of the time because his mum's never there."

She looked at her phone but there were still no messages from Jack. She tried texting him again as they walked away, hoping that this time he might answer but knowing he wouldn't.

"Let him be, Suzie. He doesn't want to speak to you, does he? What did you go and say we'd be at Joe's for?" Malky scowled.

"For Jack, you thickhead." Jenna rolled her eyes at him. "He's worried about his Gran and he's just lost everything in his house. I know what that feels like. You can't just forget it and pretend it hasn't happened, you know."

Malky shrugged as if it wasn't his concern.

"Did you see how his mum was trying to get him to meet up with us? Weird!" Suzie always felt insecure in front of Jack's mum. The woman was so perfect and Suzie knew people like that usually looked at her as if she was the scum of the earth, but today had been different.

Jenna shrugged. "Who knows? Maybe she thinks Jack might need someone to speak to. I think we should all wait for him at Joe's."

Malky made a face at her.

"He's supposed to be your best friend, Malky!"

Suzie grabbed his arm to make him stop and listen. "Jenna's right, Malky. Jack needs us just now, even if he doesn't know it."

*****

Jack hated hospitals. His abiding memory of them was from when he'd been ill as a child. He'd had to endure what had seemed like interminably long visits again and again. Sometimes, in the middle of the night, his mum had bundled him into the back seat of the car to go to the hospital, always in a panic. He remembered being sick into a bowl on the way and how the smell of it mingled with that of the disgusting air freshener his mother had kept in the car. It almost made him want to throw up just thinking about it. Then there was the revolting antiseptic smell in the hospital.

Of course when he got older Gran had explained that if it hadn't been for the doctors he might not be here today, but that didn't make it any better, he still hated going to the hospital.

Gran looked small and insignificant on the high bed, with tubes protruding from her arm and all sorts of machines buzzing and clicking beside her. She was pale and the oxygen mask covered most of her face. She could only whisper when she moved it to one side, and even that made her cough.

Jack started to feel sick. He worked his mouth, trying to avoid making a fool of himself by spewing up all over the floor. Not that his mother was aware, but he could see Gran was. She said she was tired and needed to sleep and eventually his mother took the hint. She said she had to rush back home anyway because she had a deadline to write something for the magazine, but they would come back the next day.

'Not even if Hell freezes over,' Jack muttered under his breath. It was one of Gran's favourite sayings.

*****

Jack stood at the door of Joe's Café wondering what he was doing there. He couldn't get out of the hospital quickly enough but now he felt lost. His mother had walked with him as far as the Mall and although he hadn't wanted to go, anything was better than listening to her trying to persuade him. She was going on and on about it. What made her the 'friend guru' all of a sudden?

"Jack! Hi," Suzie smiled and waved him in.

Jack looked at them all, his face wiped clear of any emotion. He walked in, kicked a chair out and sat down.

"You okay?" Suzie's voice was soft, almost a whisper. "How's your Gran? We thought..."

Jack's scowl stopped her. He pushed his hands down into his pockets and stared at the floor.

"Hey, you're just in time. Let's go and see a film." Malky's voice was cheery and sounded out of place. "There's that new horror one on. It just started this week."

"Malky!" Jenna jabbed her elbow and caught him in the ribs.

"Ow. Cut it out, Jenna. That hurt."

"Seriously, Malky. Get real." Suzie glared at him. "He doesn't want to do something like that, not just now. Do you Jack?"

"He's been wanting to see it for ages," Malky insisted. "Haven't you?"

Jack ignored them all, silently staring at the ground as if it held some fascination for him. He kept on seeing Gran, small and frail in the hospital bed with an oxygen mask covering most of her face. She had looked like a stranger. He felt lost and alone.

"Jack?" Suzie tried to take his arm.

He shrugged her off and shifted in his seat. He was inches away from her but the distance between them was a huge yawning chasm. "Just leave me, okay. Go and do whatever you want but leave me alone."

Suzie leaned forward and spoke close to his face. "We can do whatever you want, just talk to me, talk to us. We're your friends."

He ignored her. Suzie looked back at Jenna as if she might provide an answer, but she just shrugged and mouthed 'no idea'. Suzie felt helpless as she watched him hunched in his seat and switched off. Jack, the dependable one, was falling apart and she had no idea how to deal with that.

Suzie rose and headed for the toilets and Jenna stood up, nodding meaningfully at Malky before following Suzie and leaving the boys together.

*****

Suzie leaned back against the sink playing with a few strands of hair, rolling them between her fingers and jabbing the ends against her skin. "I don't know what to say to him. He won't speak to me."

She watched as Jenna carefully applied some lip gloss.

"He probably needs some time to himself, Suzie," Jenna pressed her lips together and examined the effect. "Maybe we should let him be, just for a bit."

Suzie turned back to the mirror. "Nice scarf, Jenna, is it new?" Her heart thundered in her ears. What on earth had made her say that?

Jenna looked surprised by the question. "No, I've had it for ages. Strange though, thought I'd lost it in the fire but it suddenly arrived in the post at my aunt's house this morning. There wasn't even a note with it so I have no idea who sent it."

"That's weird." Suzie was cursing her big mouth. She wondered if Jenna suspected her, and leaned down to dust imaginary specks off her jeans. "It was probably Malky!"

Jenna was now concentrating on her hair. There was hardly a strand out of place but she was carefully combing it out and flicking up the ends so that they turned out. "I asked Malky if it was him but he laughed and said why would he send it, he'd just have given it to me. Another mystery. There are too many weird things going on. I don't like it."

"Do you know if they've found out who started the fire, yet?" Suzie held her breath waiting for the answer. She wondered if the police were going to call her in again for another interview. All this waiting was doing her head in.

Jenna shook her head. "No I don't think so." Her eyes tightened and she tensed. "That detective came to the house last night. Did Jack tell you about the note?"

"What note?"

"Someone put a note through the door at my aunt's house. It was weird. Just like one of those kidnap notes you see in the films, with all the words cut out of magazines."

"No way!"

"Honestly. It said that arranged marriages were bad and that the fire was a warning."

"What did your parents say?"

"Father was upset but my aunt was fuming. She said this

proved it was something to do with me, which made her even more angry because she keeps on saying that I am bringing shame on the entire family because of the way I behave. It's not fair. But my father and my aunt don't get on. She is such a bully and she is always upsetting my mum."

"Do the police know who wrote it?"

Jenna put her comb back into her bag and closed it up again. "No, they have no idea but they took it away to get it checked by forensics. They did wonder if it could be one of my friends playing a joke." Jenna turned around to look straight at Suzie. "But it's not funny, is it?"

"Sounds crazy to me." Suzie realised that Jenna was wondering if she'd sent it. "It would be a totally stupid thing to do. Why on earth would anyone do something like that?"

Jenna looked away, seemingly satisfied. "Yeah, that's what I thought. Totally stupid."

Suzie wondered if Jenna was thinking the same as her, that it was just the kind of silly thing Malky would do, but neither of them wanted to say it out loud. She glanced at her watch. "We'd better get back out there."

CHAPTER 21

"Mrs Sorley and Jack are here, Sir."

"Bring them in, Jenny."

Larkin stood up as Jack's mother came in, followed by a cloud of her expensive perfume. He thought she looked a little less pristine and perhaps softer, or was it more weary, than the last time he'd seen her? He couldn't put his finger on it but there was something different about her. Jack looked sullen and refused to make eye contact as he slumped into the chair.

"Good Morning, Mrs Sorley, Jack." Larkin settled down and turned over one of the papers on his desk before looking up. "I have had some new evidence relating to the fire at your home."

Jack started tapping his foot against the table leg. His mother nudged him to stop. She smiled at Larkin as if to apologise. "That's excellent news." She spoke softly but with a certain arrogance that Larkin disliked. "Does that mean you know who started the fire?"

Larkin looked at Jack. Jack refused to look back at him and Larkin waited in silence for a few moments.

"Do you want to tell us about it, Jack?"

His mother looked puzzled. She stared at Jack, then she scowled at Larkin. "What do you mean?"

"Jack?" Larkin thought the boy looked ready to tell all and he wanted to give him the chance. He held up a hand to stop Mrs Sorley from interrupting. He almost felt sorry for the woman.

Jack stared at the floor. His foot was pivoting on the heel and hitting the table leg with more force each time. When he closed his eyes he could see it happening just the way it had happened that morning.

*****

She was coming home, Gran told him, but SHE hadn't told him, had she? She could have told him, spoken to him. But she really didn't care, so why should he? She was never around any more. She didn't bother to talk to him because she had other, much more important things to do.

He felt like he was watching someone else, through his own eyes; that someone else was in control of him, in control of his actions.

He was just watching.

Taking the lighter, he held it to the long strip of cloth. He waited until it had started to singe, blowing gently on the embers until they brightened. The soft glow warming the cloth was warming the bitterness in his heart, feeding the anger inside and dripping down into his belly.

He liked that warm glow, he wanted it to grow; he needed it to grow. Placing the singed cloth carefully in the cupboard he laid the silk blouse, the one he knew she treasured, so close that it would be ruined, singed and melted by the hot embers. Not enough to go on fire, just enough to destroy it. He watched the silk as it shrivelled and darkened. Then he batted at it, until it had stopped glowing and all that was left was the mess of material.

She was finally coming home and he thought about her opening the cupboard to find the charred remains of her favourite expensive blouse.

He closed the wardrobe door and pocketed the lighter as he left the house. Thinking about her reaction when she saw her ruined blouse, he smiled as he walked down the street.

The thought warmed his heart like the heat from the embers.

He had wanted to destroy something of hers, something she valued more than him. He had patted it until he had been sure the glow had disappeared and it had gone out.

*****

Larkin waited and when the silence stretched he saw Jack's mother taking a breath to say something. He frowned at her and she stopped.

Jack shrugged. "Who cares? You know, anyway."

"Why did you do it, Jack?" Larkin kept his voice quiet and encouraging.

Jack shrugged again and started kicking at the table leg once more. "Seemed like a good idea at the time."

His mother's face was a mask of horror. "*Seemed like a good idea?* Your grandmother almost died in the fire, Jack. How could you do something like that?"

Her voice triggered his anger. "What do you care? You're never here. Anyway, it wasn't meant to happen like that. It was just supposed to burn your clothes, that silk blouse you like so much. It wasn't supposed to burn down the house. I put it out. It wasn't on fire when I left."

DI Larkin took a deep breath. "It appears the embers must have smouldered away all night before it really caught hold in the middle of the morning. That's why no one noticed it. It could have flared up at any time, even during the night."

Beneath the make up, his mother's face drained of all colour.

Jack turned to her, his eyes burning holes in his head. "It wasn't supposed to hurt anyone, especially not Gran. SHE didn't deserve that..." His voice faded away, leaving the inference clear to everyone in the room. Jack dropped his head and his shoulders sagged.

Larkin had to ask the next question, even though he thought he knew the answer. "I need you to tell me about the other fire, Jack, the one in the flats. What happened there?"

It took Jack a second or two to process the question. "No way!" His cheeks flushed. "I never... I didn't... No!"

He grabbed the edge of the table with both hands, pushed his chair out behind him and stood up. He was shouting now.

"I didn't do it. You just want to pin that on me because of the other one. It wasn't me!" He looked at his mother but she was still recovering from his last admission. "It wasn't! You can't blame that on me. I wasn't in the flats that night."

Larkin could almost see the range of emotions flashing across Jack's face. He hadn't thought the boy had been the cause of the fire in the flats but he'd had to ask. Jack's reaction had been immediate and convincing.

"Okay. Take it easy." Larkin's voice was calm but commanding. "No one is trying to pin anything on you, we just need to get to the truth. Sit down so that we can talk about it. I need you to tell me what you know about that fire. Our witness said she saw you, or someone who looked like you, coming out of the flats."

Jack's mother bit her lip.

He slowly sat down and drew his chair back in a little. He swallowed and searched Larkin's face as if trying to see if he could make the man believe him. "It wasn't me! Who is the witness? I don't know who it was they saw, but it wasn't me. I have no idea who started that fire." Jack screwed up his face and turned to his mother. "I don't care whether you believe me or not. But I know I didn't do it."

CHAPTER 22

The witness

Now that the boy had gone she took a deep breath and walked up to the door of the flats. "It will be fine, it will. It will be fine, it will, it will be..."

There was a slight hesitation as she stepped inside. It was so familiar.

The hallway was in complete darkness. The lower light had failed and she remembered that it was always doing that, leaving the passage dark except for the light from the street lamps outside. Her shadow loomed ahead of her but she kept on repeating the words. "It will be fine, it will... It will be fine, it will... It will be..."

She reached the first door.

A patch of pink caught her eye, something in such contrast to the dark grey of the walls and the floor that it stood out. She went to have a look. It was just behind the caretaker's cupboard, as if it had been dropped there. A bag, a familiar bag. Her bag.

She was sure it was hers. She was very fond of that bag. Perhaps she'd had it with her and dropped it coming in. But how could that be?

She was confused. Nothing seemed right. How had her bag come to be lying here? She leaned down and picked it up but a dry skittering sound made her whirl around.

It was just a couple of dry leaves caught by the wind. But she was breathing too fast, her breath loud and rasping in her ears and all she wanted was to run away, to get as far from here as she could. She felt in her pocket for her cigarettes and quickly lit another one, drawing deeply on it, in her panic. She knew that having got this far she couldn't stop, not now. She took another deep draw to steady her nerves, and taking the first few steps to the foot of the stairs she slipped the handle of the bag across her shoulder and hugged it to her chest as a kind of security.

Staring up into the semi-darkness of the stairwell, she tried to lift her foot onto the first step but couldn't get her foot to move. She clenched her teeth and tried again, repeating and repeating the mantra." It will be fine, it will. It will be fine..."

She had done well so far but the anger, the only thing that gave her strength, had begun to diminish as she had waited outside for the boy and the girl to leave. It had dissipated like fine mist, taking her courage with it. She had thought she could do it, but she was wrong. It was too hard and she was too scared. What had happened on the street, those girls fighting and shouting at her, had shattered her fragile courage and she had nothing to rebuild it with.

Automatically lifting her hand to her lips, she drew hard on her cigarette, pulling the sharp smoke into her lungs and blowing it out again. She grabbed onto the thin metal banister.

Her nose itched with the smell, deeper than wood smoke, the smell of his clothes. Was she was imagining it? Before it had happened to him, her father had worked at the furnaces and he had always seemed to carry with him that familiar odour, regardless of how often he washed it off. It evoked in her a longing for those long lost, happy times when she had felt safe and secure. Those times when her life had been easy and she had been able to go out like everyone else, without fear, that constant companion.

It was such a strong memory that she could smell it right now but with it returned the sense of loss, isolation, and finally panic.

She'd been stupid to think she could do this. Not tonight, probably not ever. She blew at the cigarette smoke again but it seemed to be all around her. She waved it away with her hand.

It took a few moments for her to realise that there was far too much smoke for it to be coming from just one cigarette. Staring at the dimming light from the doorway, she realised that the passageway was filling up with smoke. Not just from her cigarette. Something was on fire. She peered down to the basement where the bins were but it didn't seem to be coming from there. As she turned to head back towards the exit she heard voices, deep male voices. She had to get out, right now, but they were there, outside.

She froze, clutching the banister with her one free hand and letting her cigarette end drop from between her fingers. She was no longer sure of anything, she just knew that she couldn't get trapped here. It was suddenly terrifying in the semi-darkness of the stairwell. She had to run, she had to get away.

She held on to the bag, gripping it tightly in front of her with both hands for protection, and ran, heading for the safety of the lights outside.

The smoke was thicker now as she came close to the door but she hardly noticed. Her fear had become a huge dark being, taking over her mind. She kept her eyes down, looking at her feet as they pounded the passageway, out onto the concrete path and across the grass.

She didn't look back and she didn't look up. She didn't even look around her to see if there was anyone there. She kept her head down and ran.

It had been a mistake, a huge mistake. She wasn't ready. She had to get away, to escape. She ran and ran and didn't stop until she had no breath left, then she walked quickly, gasping for breath, keeping her eyes glued to the pavement.

It was only much later when she reached the warm security of her own home, that she felt safe again. She leaned her back against the closed door, looking at the familiar, brightly lit safety of her living room and at her pink bag, lying on the sofa where she had left it.

It was a moment or two before she realised that in her arms was an identical pink bag that she was still clutching to her chest.

CHAPTER 23

Jenna stared at her father as if he had just started growing a full set of antlers, which seemed almost as likely as what she heard him saying. She heard the words but she didn't believe them. "*Jack?*" She shook her head. It made no sense at all.

"Are you sure he said Jack?"

Her father frowned. "Do you know anything about this, Jenna? How well do you know this boy?"

She shook her head. "He's one of the crowd, Father, he goes to our school but I can't believe he would do that. No, Father, he's not like that. I can't believe it. He would never do anything like that."

"Apparently he did, Jenna." Her mother turned and filled the kettle with water. "Your father told me that the police said he has already admitted that he did it."

"Seriously? It's just so unbelievable." She pulled forward a strand of her hair and combed it out between her fingers, separating the strands with her long fingernails. "... Jack?"

"The police are questioning him now, about the fire in our flat as well," her father said, his eyes fierce and dark with anger. Jenna had seen that look a lot recently. "Are you sure there is nothing you can tell us about him, Jenna?"

"No, Father, nothing. I still can't believe it. There has to be some mistake. Jack's not that kind of person."

She was desperate to call Malky and find out what he knew about it. He would know what was happening with Jack. Jenna also knew her aunt would be back home soon and she would do almost anything to avoid having to speak to the woman. She had to get away.

She looked at her watch. "Oh no, look at the time, I've got to go. I promised that I'd meet the girls at the Mall." Jenna picked up her phone as she left the room.

"Don't be late," her mother called after her. She heard her father start to speak so she hovered in the hallway for a moment, trying to overhear what he was saying. It was probably something about how she shouldn't be going out all the time. Jenna hoped her mother would back her up.

"You know the detective told us that the fire in the flats started in two places," he said.

"Two places, you mean not just in our flat?"

Jenna breathed in sharply.

"Yes, that is what he said. Another fire had been started in the basement, where the bins are kept. They think it is not very likely but it is a possibility that there were two people involved. There were two separate fires."

Her mother repeated it, as if it was beyond horror. "Two fires? But why would anyone do that?"

"He did not say." Her father, normally a quiet and calm man, had a horrible edge to his voice. "He did say that he had questioned the boy Jenna knows about the fire in our flat, to find out if he had a motive and if he might be linked to that threatening note. They think the fire was worse because one of the fires started in the rubbish bins, and that was probably why the whole building went on fire so quickly."

Jenna could hear the clink of cups as her mother poured out the tea. She heard her father blow on his, as he always did because he liked it so hot, and slurp a burning mouthful. She waited, holding her breath so that she could hear what else he might say.

"The detective told me that he doubted the boy had started those fires, but they are keeping an open mind about it. They want to know if we have any money problems, in case the fire in the basement was some kind of threat, to do with something like that."

"No!" Her mother sounded worried.

"Yes, that was what he asked. I didn't know what to tell him."

Jenna tiptoed away from the kitchen. She hated the guilty tone in her father's voice. She knew her father was as honest a man as there could be and he would have hated owing money to her aunt. She could hear the worry in her mother's voice, too. But surely her parents' problems had been solved by the fire?

Grabbing her bag she ran down the road, her head buzzing, trying to make sense of it all...

When the insurance company paid out they could repay her aunt. She had heard her father talking to the insurance company on the phone, but the company were waiting to hear if the fire had been started deliberately.

Furiously texting Malky as she walked down the road Jenna could hardly think straight, her thoughts were jumping about all over the place. She wanted to speak to him but she was still trying to understand what she had overheard.

Malky snorted as he read the text. "It's Jenna. She says she has to speak to me. 'It's urgent,' she says. With 'urgent' in capitals. Why is everything a major event with her?"

"Give her a break, Malky. She's had a hard time lately."

Malky repeated read out his reply as he was writing it. "In Mall with Suzie – will wait at Joe's."

Suzie spotted Jack at the door. "Look what the cat dragged in!" She drew a chair from the empty table next to theirs. "You look rough, where've you been? Malky's just heard from Jenna, she's on her way."

Jack slouched over and slumped into the chair, saying nothing. He didn't want to speak to anyone but he'd had nowhere else to go. He certainly didn't want to go back to the B & B and have to talk to his mother.

"Look, here's Jenna, now. She looks worse than you, Jack. Like she's seen a ghost."

CHAPTER 24

Jenna was standing at the door of the café, staring at them. "Jack?" She stepped forward, frowning at him. "What did..? How did..?"

"What's going on, Jenna?" Malky asked. "Sounded like it was something pretty important."

Jenna approached the table looking as if she wanted to strangle Jack.

She ignored both Malky and Suzie, and when she spoke, it was directly to Jack.

"Why? Why would you do that? What did I do to you?" She leaned across the table, inches from his face." How could you?"

Jack just stared down at his hands, refusing to look at her.

"Lay off, Jenna. What's going on?" Suzie pulled at Jack's arm, but he shrugged her off. " Jack? What's she on about? What did you do?"

Jenna turned to face her, flushed with fury and shining with tears, then returned her attention to Jack. "Yes, why don't you tell them, Jack?" She poked the air in front of Jack with her finger. "Tell them how you burned out our flat, and almost killed that family."

Suzie was on her feet yelling back at her. "No! Jack would never do anything like that. He wouldn't. Tell her, Jack."

Jack sat there, his head dropping into his hands.

"Jack? You didn't ...Jack?" Her voice dwindled to a whisper. "Did you?"

"Why haven't they arrested you?" Jenna stood back upright again, still glaring at him across the table. "You should be locked up. I hope they put you away forever."

He was shaking his head and at first Suzie thought he might

be crying. "I didn't go near your flat, Jenna." His voice was grey and flat as if he could hardly get the words out. "It was *my* house, not yours. The police said I would be charged later, and I could go home as long as I came back in tomorrow."

Malky's face was flushed in places and drained of colour in others. "*You* did it? You set your *own* house on fire?"

Suzie sank back into her seat. "But your Gran? Jack you love your Gran and she almost died in the fire."

Jack turned on her, fury etched on his face. "Don't you think I know that? Do you really think I wanted that to happen? It was an accident, a mistake. I didn't mean anyone to get hurt. I just... Oh, forget it, you wouldn't understand."

"Try me," Suzie whispered. "We're your friends." She glared at Jenna, who sat down looking only slightly embarrassed by her outburst and much more like her usual controlled self.

"Jenna was just being..." Suzie couldn't find the right word, one that wouldn't start another fight. "Jenna... You know she didn't mean it, Jack."

Jack started digging at the polystyrene coffee cup with his nails, gouging out little pieces and flicking them across the table. "It was stupid, a stupid mistake. I just wanted to destroy something of hers, something she cared about."

Malky made a face. "Why would you want to destroy something that belonged to your Gran?"

Suzie rolled her eyes. "Get with the programme, Malky. It was something belonging to his mother, obviously, not his Gran."

Jack nodded. "I'd heard she was coming home but she didn't even bother to tell me that she wasn't staying, that she was only going to be home for a couple of days and then she had some fancy thing to go to in Paris. She never thought it important enough to tell me, she just told Gran, because I don't matter, do I?"

He pressed his nail into the cup, as if it was penetrating skin and flesh. "I left a smouldering rag beside her favourite silk blouse. I thought I had put it out. It was the night of the blaze in your flat, Jenna. It must have smouldered for ages before it caught fire the next morning.

"I never thought it would set the whole place on fire. I didn't. Really I didn't. I thought it would just singe things a bit. It wasn't meant to happen like that. I wouldn't do something like that."

"See." Suzie looked at them all in turn, her gaze finally settling on Jenna. "I told you. It was an accident. It was a mistake. And he didn't set your flat on fire. Did you Jack?"

He shook his head "Jenna. I'd never do that."

"How did you find out about Jack, Jenna?" Malky was still looking shocked and pale. "Did the police tell you? Have they any other suspects? Do they know anything more about the fire in the flats?"

Jenna was secretly pleased that Malky was so interested. Up until now he'd hardly seemed to care very much. "My dad asked me if I knew Jack, and he told me what the police had said about him setting fire to his own house." Her voice dropped to almost a whisper, as if she didn't want Jack to hear it. "And he said that if you'd done that at your own home you might easily have been the one who set fire to our flat, too."

"MIGHT have!" Suzie barked at her. "They only said MIGHT have done it. You came in here and accused him of setting fire to the flats, of almost being a murderer. I know for a fact that Jack couldn't have set the flats on fire because he was with me all the time. So there! You could have just asked. You should watch who you accuse of things, Jenna."

Jenna flushed. "I'm sorry. I suppose I was just angry about it all and didn't think that clearly. But if Jack was with you all the time surely the police know that? So why would they suspect him?"

Suzie bit her lip. She knew he hadn't been with her all the time, but when she was in the flats Jack had been away looking for her jacket, so she knew he couldn't have done it then because he'd have had to get past her. However, it struck her that if the fire in his own house had smouldered all night before it went up he could have gone to the flats before he came to meet them at the corner.

She didn't mention that the police had said the witness had seen her and Jack coming out of the flats. Anyway that had to be rubbish, Jack hadn't been there. But had the witness seen someone else, then? Or had the witness seen Jack earlier in the evening?

When she thought about it like that it was really strange. She had been in the flats, but Jack hadn't. So who was the other person the witness saw?

CHAPTER 25

"Do they have any other suspects for the fire in the flat, then, Jenna?" Malky asked. "Did they say anything else about it?"

"It's all a bit confusing." Jenna bit her lip. "My father didn't tell me much more but I did overhear him and mum speaking and he told her that there had been two fires and they were still trying to work out which had been started first. It could be that one of them had been a professional job."

"What does that mean?" Malky snapped. "Are they looking for professionals then? Who sets fire to a place 'professionally'? Is that like a hitman, was it a professional 'hit'? Is it something to do with your family, then? Would someone have put a contract out on them?"

Jenna scowled at him. "Seriously, Malky? Everything doesn't have to be like it is on TV. This is real."

Suzie was watching Malky closely. He and Jenna didn't normally snipe at each other all the time. "He probably means some thugs were trying to get protection money," Suzie suggested. "But if they think that only one of the fires was started by a professional... does that mean the other was amateur, so are they looking for different people?"

"Well, it wasn't me!" Jack stared at Jenna as if he could make her believe him through force of will alone. "You know me well enough to know that I wouldn't do something like that, Jenna."

"How do I know that, Jack? You've just said you set your own place alight. Do you expect me to believe that you would do that to your own home but not to mine?" Jenna's eyes filled up. "I'm sorry, Jack, I didn't really mean that but I just don't know what to believe anymore."

"It's not that we don't want to believe you, Jack," Malky

butted in. "But she has a point."

Suzie thought Malky seemed almost too eager. Was he just trying to pacify Jenna?

Jack crushed the cup in his hand and turned to Suzie. "I suppose you think I did it, too, then?"

Suzie was shocked into silence. She was so surprised to see the ever-dependable Jack falling apart that she just sat there unable to frame a sentence. He was so angry; she'd never seen him like this. This wasn't the Jack she knew, the Jack she needed, the one who did things right.

Like a chill running right through her she realised that she needed Jack to be strong. He was the person she needed as her support, someone she could hold up as a solid person when her life went crazy. She felt a crushing disappointment that he wasn't the person she needed him to be.

Almost as quickly as the thought appeared she began to feel ashamed and selfish but she didn't know what to do. She wasn't used to being a support for someone else. She wasn't sure she knew how. Jack needed her but was she ready to be that person?

Jack was looking at her, waiting for her to back him up, to tell them all that she knew he wasn't involved in the fire at the flats. But in that moment of hesitation, her silence was too long.

"Typical. I thought at least you..." He stared at her with that look she hated. The look that said she had failed and disappointed him, that she was no more than she appeared, she was just like everyone said she was.

"Jack, I'm sorry I ..."

He turned away, but not before she had seen all his hurt, anger and disillusionment. Jack turned back and glared at her. "I suppose you don't want to tell us what exactly you were doing in the flats before the fire, do you Suzie? When you'd sent me off to get your jacket? I saw you coming out of the flats. Want to tell us what exactly you were up to? You've never liked Jenna. Maybe *you* were the one who started it?"

Suzie blushed scarlet.

How could Jack say that? He was the one on her side. He was the person who looked out for her, kept her secrets. How could he accuse her like that? But she could see in his eyes that he didn't know if he could trust her. That he'd been asking himself that very question all along.

All this time he really thought she might have done it but had been covering for her. With her silence she had destroyed that trust. He'd said it out loud and now the others would blame her, too. She couldn't drag her eyes from Jack and she didn't dare look at Jenna.

"No," she wanted to shout but her voice failed her. "It wasn't like that. I didn't..." Her stomach felt like lead. She now knew no one would believe anything she said.

"How could you, Suzie?" Malky jumped in. His tone was righteous, condemning her.

She had thought he was her friend, too. She'd known him for years and thought he understood her. Why was he trying to make her look bad? What had she done to him? Suzie turned to Malky, spitting fury and venom. "You know it wasn't me. Maybe it was you!" she snapped at him.

"Oh, that's rich," Jenna cut in. "You've been caught and now you're trying to pin the blame on Malky. You disgust me, Suzie. I had begun to think you might not be as bad as they said you were, but seems I was wrong. Next you'll be saying *I* did it."

"No! It wasn't me. Malky, tell her it wasn't me, tell her the truth." But a glance in his direction showed her that Malky was not going help her. Not now, not ever.

She got up and grabbed her coat. "You all make me sick. Yes, blame the bad girl. That never gets old, does it?" She leaned across the table so that her face was close to Malky's. "But you and I know that's what happens all the time. I thought at least *you* might stick up for me!"

They watched in silence as Suzie stomped off.

"So now at least we know who set fire to your place, Jenna." Malky seemed almost smug about it. "Do you think we should tell the police?"

"Malky!" Jack yelled across the table at him. You are a complete prat. You know Suzie wouldn't do something like that."

"You were the one who said it, Jack. Changed your mind now, have you? Well it's too late. You said you saw her coming out of the flats. Why else was she there? You know she was jealous of me and Jenna."

Jack shook his head. "She didn't give a toss about you and Jenna. You're delusional, Malky, and stupid with it. If you go to the police I'll just deny it. Suzie didn't do it."

Jenna looked at Malky and then at Jack, and back at Malky. "Shut up! Just shut up, both of you."

Silence rippled out from the table and across the café.

*****

Suzie leaned against the wall, struggling to keep it together. She wiped the back of her hand across her cheek to obliterate the tears she hadn't been able to contain, and sniffed, biting her lips hard.

Jack had betrayed her. She had seen how they'd all looked at her, the horror on their faces, even Jack's. How could he do that? A small inner voice tried to reason that she hadn't backed him up either. But that had been a moment of complete shock when she had realised he was not denying that he'd started the fire in his own house.

She knew it was all about his mother. He was always so angry with her. But she still couldn't get over that Jack would actually do something like that. It seemed so out of character. He was the 'good' one, the sensible one who kept Malky from being stupid, and kept her together. She felt betrayed by that almost as much as by his accusation that she started the fire in Jenna's flat. How could he do that to her? But then, why should he be any different than anyone else? She should have known better than to believe he was her friend.

Then there was Malky. She had realised, in that moment when she had confronted him, that Malky knew she was going into the flats that night.

When she heard her phone ring tone, Suzie hoped it was Jack, but she was far too angry to speak to him, so she let it ring. Eventually it went off and she had a look. It wasn't Jack after all, it was her foster mother. There was nothing she could have to say that Suzie wanted to hear.

She pushed the phone back into her pocket with a sniff and wiped her eyes again as she set off down the road. She had half hoped that Jack would come after her or at least call or text her, but now she was beginning to get angry that he hadn't. He was probably glad to get rid of her anyway, she told herself, so why would she want to speak to him.

She didn't need him. She didn't need any of them, did she?

CHAPTER 26

DI Larkin decided to call Suzie's foster mother again. He needed to speak to the girl and he didn't want to wait much longer. He felt as if it was all beginning to come together and he had a gut feeling that if a couple of little things fell into place the whole picture would become clear. The number rang out for a while and just as he was about to ring off she answered.

"Hello?"

"It's DI Larkin. I spoke to you earlier. I was just wanting to confirm that you are going to bring Suzie in for another interview this afternoon?"

"Yes, so you did. Well, she's just come in. I've been calling her all morning. Never tells me where she's going, this one. When do you want to speak to her?"

"As soon as possible." Larkin sighed. "That would be good."

"We're just having some lunch so I suppose I could bring her in after that," she said, grudgingly. "It's not as if I have anything else to do!"

Larkin bit his tongue on a sharp reply and forced himself to be polite. "Thank you, I appreciate that you are busy, but I am sure you realise that this is a serious matter."

Things were piling up. He supposed it was just going to be one of those days. Larkin wanted to make sure he could place where each of the four teenagers had been before the fire was reported that night. Now that he had more of a picture of things he knew what questions he needed to ask. It was always a bit like this, fishing around in the dark for answers at first before it began to fall into place. The trick was not forcing pieces of the jigsaw to fit just because it was convenient and he had a bit of a feeling that there was something else going on here that he didn't quite understand.

He had asked Malky's mother to bring him back in and had spoken to Jack already, and that left Jenna. Larkin wasn't sure Jenna's father was being completely honest with him; his instincts told him there was something he didn't want Larkin to find out about.

A knock at the door roused him from his thoughts

"I thought you might like a coffee, Sir."

Larkin looked at the cup in her hand and smiled. "Jenny, you are a life saver!"

"We've just had a call from the psychiatrist, Dr Hopper. I'd asked her for a report on the witness, Janice. She said Janice called her last night saying she had something to show us, some material evidence but that she didn't want to come back in to the station. Dr Hopper said it would be too traumatic for her and she wondered if we could send someone round. She feels Janice would be more receptive to that and we might get a more coherent response in her home surroundings."

She put the mug of coffee on his desk. "I could go to see her if you like. She seems comfortable with me." She placed a typed sheet on his desk beside the coffee. "And I thought you would want to see this right away. It's from forensics."

He knew the young WPC was incredibly keen to work on this case. She was bright, curious and paid great attention to detail, which was just what was required.

"Yes, thanks, good idea. Why don't you go around to her place this morning and collect whatever it is she's got. See if you can get some sense out of her about who she saw that night."

Larkin sat back in his chair, deep in thought, reading the note from forensics. Something had just occurred to him. It might be nothing, but better to be sure.

CHAPTER 27

Malky slammed the door and stomped up the stairs to his room.

"Malky?" his mother called up from the kitchen. "Is that you? Don't slam the door, dear."

Who else did she think it was, the Green Giant? He had been about to slam the door of his bedroom and thought about doing it just to annoy her but it wasn't worth the hassle. He threw himself on his bed.

He'd been hoping to spend some time with Jenna, he'd hardly seen her lately but she said she had to go home. When he complained that she never wanted to be with him she lost her temper and stormed off. He had almost told her what he'd done to make it all right for the two of them to be together, but he wasn't sure how she'd react. She had been acting all weird lately.

"Malky." His mother knocked on his door.

"Leave me alone, Mum. I'm tired."

"Malky, can I come in? I need to speak to you."

"Aww, Mum. Leave it, will you. I'm really not in the mood. Can't it wait till later?" Never, was what he really meant.

He heard the door handle turning. It squeaked as it turned, and that was just one other thing he hated. If his dad was around he would soon sort the handle. His dad had been good like that, always fixing things. That was what he remembered most about his dad. But his mum had constantly whined at him and she was always having one of her 'turns', which meant she couldn't cook or do the washing or clean the house or pretty much anything other than mess about with her hair or watch her favourite soaps on TV, so it had meant his dad had to do everything.

His dad left them when Malky was quite young. He had ended up in care for a while because his mother suffered some kind of breakdown. His dad had come back but it hadn't worked and he'd left again soon after. For as long as Malky could remember his dad had come and gone but never stayed more than a few months before leaving again. Sometimes he hadn't come back for a couple of years. When his mother had told him his dad had left for good Malky hadn't believe her at first, but she'd been right. His dad never came back. He didn't really blame his dad for leaving, his mother could be a right pain, and sometimes he wished he could leave too. But he had nowhere to go and he had no idea where his dad was, so that wasn't an option.

"Why do you bother knocking, if you're just going to come in anyway?"

Her face bore that pathetic expression. She thought it made people feel sorry for her. She didn't seem to realise it wasn't going to work with him, he knew her too well. It was just her way to get what she wanted and make it look like she was being nice all the time.

Malky groaned and grabbed his pillow, holding it over his face so he didn't have to look at her. "What is it?" he mumbled through the padding.

"I got a call today." She waited.

"Good for you."

"It was that nice police detective, what was his name? Larking, I think. The handsome one we went to speak to last time."

Malky froze behind the pillow, waiting for her to get to the point, but she had stopped talking. He slowly edged the pillow down until he could see what her expression was like. The blood was rushing, crashing in his ears with the roar of a waterfall. It was almost louder than he could bear. Why had the police called? All the possibilities were chasing through his head. Had someone seen him?

He swallowed and it felt like he had a walnut stuck in his throat. "What did he want?"

"Oh, don't look so worried. I am sure it was nothing really. He wants us to come in and have another little chat with him. He thinks you might be able to tell him a bit more about that terrible fire. He said it's just in case there is something you saw that may not have seemed important at the time but could help them find out who did it."

"I don't know anything. There's no point. You can just tell him that, Mum."

She shook her head and smiled at him, as if he was still about five years old. "Now there's nothing to look so worried about, dear." She sat down beside him and patted his hand. He pulled it away from her. "I told him we would come in later on this afternoon, about three o'clock. You can just tell him you don't remember anything else, when we get there. Anyway, you saw how attentive he was to me when we went met him last time. I think he actually quite likes me!"

Malky groaned again. Why couldn't he have a normal mother, someone on the same planet as everyone else? She simply had no idea, no idea at all.

She got up and started smiling at herself in the 007 novelty mirror on his wall. It didn't seem to matter to her that she could hardly see more than a bit of her face in it at one time in the tiny bit of mirror between James Bond and his Walther PPK.

She patted her hair into place and turned back to face him. "Now, Malky, you'd better get yourself washed and tidied up. You can't go to the police station dressed in those old clothes.

We'll need to leave in about an hour and a half."

"But Mum..."

"Malcolm!"

Malky shook his head. He knew that when she called him by his full name it was a kind of code that meant she was not going to give in to an argument. He hated that she thought this was such a clever thing to do, but he also knew there was no point in saying anything. He just wanted to get her out of his room so that he could have some peace to think straight.

He stood up and dropped the pillow back on his bed. "Okay, Mum. I'll get changed."

She was still standing there.

"Right now!" He glared at her.

"Oh, yes." She seemed surprised by the sudden lack of resistance. "That's fine. Well, look at the time. I'd better get myself all prettied up."

As soon as she left, Malky sank back onto his bed.

Why did the police want to speak to him again? He knew well enough, even if his mother didn't, that it was nothing to do with her. Was it the note? What if they knew that he'd sent it. Perhaps someone in the house had seen him putting it through the letterbox?

No, he was sure no one had seen him that night apart from those two guys, and they had just passed him by.

What if they had done some clever forensic stuff and found out that way? He couldn't remember what exactly he had told them the first time but he didn't think he'd said anything much, and if he remembered it right the detective had been more interested in Jenna and her family, especially the cousins.

Maybe he could put them 'in the frame'. He liked using phrases like that, the kind TV cops used. It made him feel important and intelligent. The idea seemed to grow in his head. It seemed better and better. That's what he would do. He would have to be clever today and watch what he said, if he wanted to blame the fire on Jenna's cousins. He'd have to drop clues but not be too obvious about it.

His phone jangled, announcing a text message. It was Jenna.

Need 2 see U NOW! parents - in melt down. Meet me @ corner in 10 min. PLS COME! Xx

She had been so angry with him when she'd left Joe's that this had to be something major to get her so upset.

no prob

he texted, looking at his watch. He had to get out of the house before his mother stopped him. Grabbing his jacket and a half eaten bar of chocolate he'd just spotted lying under his bed, he ran downstairs and opened the front door.

"Malky! Where are you going?" His mother shrieked down at him, her head poking out of her bedroom door. "You can't go out now, we have to go to the police station!"

"We don't have to be there for ages, Mum." He tried to sound calm but he was desperate to get along to meet Jenna. He didn't want her thinking he wasn't coming, especially when she sounded so upset. He never knew what she was going to do next and if he wasn't there she would probably never forgive him. "I'll meet you at the police station, mum."

"No, you won't. You just stay here so I know where you are. If you go running off you'll forget the time or something. I don't want you to be late."

"I won't, Mum. Look I've got to go out for a bit. I'll meet you there at 3pm, on the dot. I promise." He knew she was not pleased but he was already closing the door as she called down.

"You'd better be there, Malky, and don't you dare be late!"

CHAPTER 28

Malky ran down towards the corner where his street met the main road. Jenna was standing in a shop doorway waiting for him. Her eyes were puffy and red and she had a large bag with her.

"Thought you weren't coming."

"Oh, Babe. I said I would, didn't I?" He put an arm around her and pulled her close. He could feel her shoulders shaking as she leaned in towards him and sobbed.

"It was horrible, Malky. I have never seen them so angry."

"C'mon, let's get out of here." He guided her away from the busy street and prying eyes and headed towards the park.

The park was busy with families and joggers but he led her along one of the quieter paths and found a bench a little out of the way. It was shrouded by trees, which gave them a sense of privacy.

"So what on earth happened?" he asked. She had stopped crying and seemed a little calmer.

"It was my aunt. She's such a bully. She was insisting that my parents do everything just the way she wants it. She says that I am causing shame to the family because of the way I dress and the way I behave, that it is not only affecting our family but hers too. She was furious when I said I wasn't going to marry Pavan and that she couldn't make me.

'She said that it was making us less respected in the community and she had her reputation to think of, that she had worked so hard to make this happen and she wasn't letting a silly girl destroy all that."

"But they can't force you to do it. It's the twenty-first century, that shouldn't happen."

Jenna sniffed and wiped a tear away with the back of her

hand. "I know it shouldn't, but it does. And I'm scared. My father was so angry with her, at first, then she said something quietly to him, I couldn't hear it and he stopped. The next thing I knew he seemed to be angry with me. He's never like this. I just don't understand why he is still listening to her and letting her dictate what he does. It makes no sense."

"Didn't your mum stand up for you?"

"That's strange, too. It's as if my aunt has some hold over them. I think it might be something to do with some money she gave my father, but I thought that was all sorted. The insurance from the fire will be more than enough to repay her so I don't understand why they still won't stand up to her. But what was even more frightening was that she said she is head of the family now my uncle is dead, and if my parents don't do something to make me fall into line, she'll have her sons do what she thinks is needed."

Malky frowned at her. "What? Was she threatening you, then?"

She looked solemnly into his eyes and he could see how scared she was. "I think so, I wasn't sure at first but then my mother started sobbing and crying, which is just not like her. That was when I knew I had to get away. I think she means to send the cousins after me and it has my parents scared stiff, so it's not an idle threat. Oh, Malky. I am so frightened."

Malky hugged her closer as she dissolved into tears again.

"Will you come away with me?" Her eyes were dark and pleading. "We could go far away to some big city where they will never find me. I've got some money." She clutched at the bag on the seat beside her. "I've got some money I took before the fire, so no one knows I have it. I feel bad about taking it, but we'll need it to pay for somewhere to stay."

"You want me to run away with you?" Malky was trying to

get his head around the idea.

Jenna looked up warily at him and started to chew on the nail of her little finger, waiting to see how he would react. "You will you come with me, Malky. Won't you?"

"Of course! What a stupid question."

"I was going to ask you that, on the night of the fire." She nibbled on her nail again and hesitated, still unsure of him.

"You were? Why didn't you tell me?"

"I met my cousins coming into the flat as I was leaving and I hid my bag in the hallway because I didn't want them asking too many questions about it. But when I saw you with Suzie... I was really angry and upset because I thought you didn't care about me at all."

"Your cousins were there that night? At the flat, before the fire started? I thought they would have been at your big family party?"

She shook her head. "They asked me why I wasn't at the party and what I was doing. I told them that what I did was my own business." She was quiet for a moment. "I wonder why they were there? I haven't thought about that before, I was so busy trying to hide my bag and get away so that they wouldn't notice it."

"So it could have been your cousins who started the fire?"

Jenna stopped and thought about that for a moment. "The note!" she squealed.

Malky drew in a breath and held it. Did she know? He was so busy trying to think of a way to explain it to her that he almost didn't hear her next words.

"They must have sent the note! They were probably trying to make it seem like it was someone else." She grabbed his arm, looking quite horrified. "Malky, I just realised. They were probably trying to frame you for the fire!"

Malky opened his mouth and shut it again. The pure simplicity and plausibility of her reasoning were amazing and exactly what he needed. If he told the police all this, they would be completely off his case and the cousins would get the blame for the fire. He grabbed Jenna and pulled her to him.

"You are so clever!" He drew in the special scent of her and nuzzled her neck. "I can tell the police all this when I see them this afternoon."

Jenna pushed him away. "You're going to the police? Today? I thought you were coming away with me?"

"I have to go. They asked my mother to bring me in again. They want to ask more questions about the night of the fire."

"What else can you tell them that they don't know already? Is there something else, Malky?"

"There was this witness and she saw me and Suzie coming out of the flats."

Jenna's face clouded with suspicion. "You were with Suzie?"

"No, no. Not together. Suzie was with Jack, you know that."

"So Jack was in the flats too?"

Malky grabbed both her hands and held them to calm her enough so he could tell his side of the story. "Suzie had some photos. Ones she took at Sam's party last week. She'd had copies made and she'd told me she was going to post them through your door so that your dad would see them."

Jenna drew her hands away and clenched both fists. "That sneaky, nasty bitch! Dad would go mental!"

"Exactly. So, after you went off, I wanted to try and stop her doing it. But by the time I got there Suzie was just coming out. She met up with Jack and they went off. So I went inside to see if I could get the photos, in case she had left them stuck in the letterbox or something. But she had put them right through and I could see them lying on the floor inside. There was nothing I could do. So I went to try and find you, to tell you."

"And that was when the witness saw you coming out?" Malky took a breath. She believed him, so the police would too.

Jenna thought for a moment. "Malky?"

The questions in her voice sent a shock of panic through him. "What?"

"Did you see the cousins at the flats at all. When you were there? Could they have been hanging around waiting to start the fire?"

Malky shook his head. He could reply with absolute honesty to this one. "No, Jenna, I never saw them at all that night. But I wasn't there long and they could have come into the flats after I left. Yes, that's probably exactly what happened."

"Do you really have to go back to the police station? Can't we just leave right now?"

"I promised I'd meet my mum there about 3pm. If I don't turn up she'll raise the alarm and they'll be looking for us right away. We need some time to get far enough away so that they won't find us."

"But I don't know where to go. I'm scared my cousins may already be looking for me."

He reached for her hand again. "We can find a safe place for you to wait for me, somewhere no one will look for you, then I can meet you there afterwards."

Malky thought for a moment. "I think I know a place. It's a bit of a mess, but no one would think of looking for you there."

CHAPTER 29

DI Larkin had just finished a fairly tasteless cheese sandwich from the police station cafeteria when he got a message to say that his first appointment of the afternoon had arrived. Swallowing down a gulp of tea he left the remains of his lunch with little regret. He promised himself a decent meal at Mario's, his favourite Italian restaurant, if he got clear in time. But there was no guarantee of that.

He entered the interview room and sat down opposite Suzie, trying to ignore the scowl she threw in his direction. Suppressing a sigh of irritation he opened the conversation with a smile.

"Hello again, Suzie. Thank you both for coming in at such short notice but we are close to solving this case and we need to find the perpetrator as soon as possible so that no one else gets hurt."

"Looking to blame me then?"

"No, Suzie. I'm not looking for someone to blame, I want to find out the truth. It helps no one if we put away the wrong person and the arsonist strikes again, does it?"

Suzie shrugged. She looked down and started picking at her nails.

Larkin waited and let the silence grow. Suzie's foster mother began to fidget and shift in her seat restlessly. Just before she started to say something about him wasting her time, he spoke again.

"Suzie. Can you tell me why you were in Marling Street on Wednesday night?"

She tensed, looking straight at him, refusing to answer.

"Suzie, this is important. Jenna's family have been staying there since the fire, I am sure you know that, don't you."

"So what if I do? I thought it was a free country. I can go where I like."

"Can you tell me what you were doing there?"

She shrugged again and muttered something he couldn't hear.

"I'm sorry, I can't hear you."

"Speak up, Suzie, this is ridiculous. You're just being childish," her foster mother snapped. "Stop wasting everyone's time and tell the detective why you were there. What were you up to?"

With a glare Suzie slumped back into her seat. "I wasn't 'up to' anything, I just went to see if she was in." "But you didn't go to the door, did you?"

She leaned forward again and with both hands on the desk said, "How do you know what I did or didn't do? Am I being followed or summat?"

They had hardly enough manpower to do the job much less follow teenagers around all day. Larkin let a small smile cross his face at the idea.

"As it happens I was on my way to speak to the family. I saw you come along the road, but then you turned back. What were you planning to do, Suzie? Was it you that sent that note to Jenna's father, about arranged marriages?"

It was Suzie's turn to laugh. "Why would I do that? None of my business who they make her marry. It's a bit rubbish though, I'd never let anyone do that to me."

"So you heard about the note, then?"

"Yeah. Jenna told us. Seems a stupid thing to do. Like advertising that he had set the place on fire."

Larkin was suddenly alert. "You said 'he'. Do you know who started the fire in the flat, Suzie? It's really important so think for a moment before you answer. Remember the little baby you caught that night. Without you saving her, she would have died. Her mother is very ill because of that fire. She almost died, too."

Suzie looked to the side, avoiding his eyes. She was cursing herself for letting that slip out but she wasn't ever going to finger him for it. Anyway she couldn't be sure, could she? It probably wasn't him at all.

After a short pause she shook her head firmly. "It was just a slip of the tongue. How would I know who did it?"

As she said it she suddenly remembered they might be thinking it was Jack. "It wasn't Jack!" She had almost shouted it out and quickly brought her voice down a pitch or two.

Raising an eyebrow Larkin spoke in a level tone. "How can you be sure it wasn't Jack?"

"Because he was with me all the time and he was never in the flats at all."

"You know we have a witness who says you were both there. That she saw you both coming out of the flats."

"Well, that's just rubbish!" She was angry now. "Jack never went near the flats, he was with me, and that's the truth."

"But you did?" Larkin slipped it in quickly, hoping for a rapid and truthful response. Suzie flushed and he could see her trying to think of a way out of it.

"You were in the flats, but Jack wasn't? Is that how it was? What were you doing there, Suzie? I know you and Jenna weren't friends. Did you start the fire, Suzie?"

"NO!" she shrieked back at him. "I didn't start the fire! Okay, I was in the flats but that's not what I was doing. It wasn't me."

"All right, all right, I want to believe you." He held her eyes trying to make her trust what he said. "Just tell me what you were doing in the flats. But I want the whole truth, now."

Suzie felt caught, trapped, but for some reason she believed him. "I sent Jack off to look for my jacket," she told him. She began to laugh at herself. "I thought he wouldn't approve of what I was going to do. Him! I really thought he was 'Mister too-good-to-be-true'. The joke was on me, wasn't it?"

"So what was it that you were going to do, Suzie? What was it you thought Jack wouldn't approve of?"

Suzie took a deep breath. It was time to tell the whole story.

CHAPTER 30

As she was leaving the interview room Suzie pulled out her phone and started to tap in Jack's number.

"Stop that for a moment, Suzie. We need to have a little chat." Her foster mother sounded irritated and the last thing Suzie could face right now was a lecture. She made a face but her foster mother was looking at the sign above her head. "Oh, actually, I'll be back in a minute, Suzie. Just wait here, will you," she said, veering off towards the toilets.

Suzie sat down to wait on one of the seats in the corridor. She was about to call Jack again when a couple came in and walked past her. DI Larkin left the interview room and walked up to them.

"Mr & Mrs Chowdhury. Thank you for coming in."

It was Jenna's parents. She watched them follow Larkin to his office. Through the open door Suzie could see that there was a large pink bag on his desk. Suzie recognised it instantly because she had often wished she'd had one just like it but knew she could never have afforded it.

"That's Jenna's bag!" Mrs Chowdhury cried out, as soon as she saw it. "It's Jenna's! How did you get it? Why is it here? Is she here? Where is she?"

"Are you quite sure it's hers, Mrs Chowdhury?" Larkin's voice was calm and soothing.

Reaching over she lifted a keyring with a small dog on it. "See, this is hers, it even has her initials on it. It's the one she was always losing, so I said to her she should attach it to her bag. Why is it here? Jenna said it was destroyed in the fire. It was one of the things she was upset about losing."

Her husband scowled at Larkin. "Why do you have Jenna's bag? Has something happened to her?" He turned to his wife.

"I told you she had run away!"

At that point the door of the interview room was closed, leaving Suzie desperate to find out more. There were too many people coming and going. She could hardly go over and listen at the door.

She had to go and find Jack and Malky, they would know what was happening. With a glance down the corridor she checked there was no sign of her foster mother. If she waited she would have to listen to another lecture and she wouldn't get away for ages.

Suzie slipped out of the front door of the police station and ran down the road towards Joe's, tapping Jack's number on her phone as she went.

His phone rang several times before he answered it.

"Jack! Jack I need to speak to you. Where are you?" She was relieved that he had actually answered. It meant he was still speaking to her. She'd not even been sure he would answer her calls.

"Suzie? What's up?"

"Where are you? I've got to speak to you. Is Malky with you?"

"No, he went off with Jenna this morning and I've not seen him since. I'm about half way down the High Street. What's going on, Suzie, are you okay?"

"I'll meet you there. I'll tell you when I see you. I won't be long. Wait for me."

Suzie ran down the street, thrusting her phone back in her pocket as she went. The traffic was heavy and, as she waited to cross the road, she tried to make sense of what she had overheard and of why the police had Jenna's bag? The questions rattled around her head but she couldn't think straight. She had to tell Jack that she'd made sure the police knew he'd not had anything to do with the fire at the flats.

But at the back of her mind she still had...a feeling. It was just like having a stone caught in her shoe, it irritated and kept coming back to pester her. She didn't want to believe it but the longer it rolled about in her head the more it bothered her. She had to speak to Malky.

*****

"Jack!"

Jack turned to see Malky running down the street towards him. Malky leaned one hand against the shop window, trying to catch his breath.

"You need to get in shape!"

Malky shook his head, as if that was irrelevant. "Jack, you got some cash?" he gasped.

"What? What for?"

"It's Jenna. We've got to get out of here, stat! Her aunt has sent her cousins after her because she won't marry that guy her family chose for her. She's terrified."

"Seriously? This isn't another one of your jokes is it?" Jack knew, even as he said it, that Malky wasn't fooling about.

Malky shook his head. "This is dead serious, mate. Jenna is hiding in that old wreck of a house down Gravel Street, until I get back. But we need some cash and I've only got a few quid. Can you lend me some, just until we get sorted out a bit? I'll pay you back. I will."

"You know I would, Malky, but I'm pretty short myself. I can probably only stretch to about 10 quid. I thought Jenna's family were loaded."

Malky made a face. "She's got some but it isn't all that much. I've got a little but it won't get us very far."

Jack thought for a moment. "Look, if you're really stuck I could probably get a bit more, but I'll need to get to a cash machine first."

"Ace! Thanks mate. There's one just down there." Malky started to walk away but Jack hadn't moved. "C'mon, Jack, What you waiting for?"

Jack shook his head. "Hold on. I can't go yet. Suzie's on her way to meet me here. Look, there she is."

"Jack!" Suzie ran the last few yards. "Malky, thank goodness you're here, too. Where's Jenna? Do you know where she is?"

Malky scowled at her suspiciously. "Why?"

"I've just come from the police station and her parents were there. They said she had run away."

"If they know about Jenna her cousins probably do, too. I'd better get back to her." Malky looked at his watch and swore. "I'm supposed to be meeting my mum at the police station right now. Have you got any spare cash, Suzie?"

Suzie laughed. "Yeah right, as if I've ever had wads of cash lying about. Don't be stupid, Malky." She turned to Jack. "Look, I told the police about that night, Jack, that you were with me and you couldn't have started the fire at the flats. It puts you in the clear."

"Thanks." He looked deep into her eyes. "Suz, I really didn't mean what I said earlier today."

"It's okay, I told them why I was in the flats." Jack looked as if he was holding his breath, waiting to hear what she was going to say next. "It wasn't anything to do with the fire. It was the photos. The ones I took of Jenna at Sam's party."

She shrugged, unable to meet his eyes. "Look, I'm not proud of myself, but I wanted to get Jenna into trouble. I wanted to show Malky that she was just playing him along then she was going to do exactly what her family wanted." She sneaked a look at Malky but his expression was unreadable.

"I put them through the letterbox. Didn't think you would approve so that was why I sent you off to get my jacket."

Jack took a deep breath. "Did you see anyone else there? Do you know who started the fire?"

Malky butted in quickly before Suzie could say anything. "Jenna and I worked out who it was. It was her cousins. I was going to tell the cops all about it, today, but I can't go now. I've got to get back to Jenna. Jack c'mon. Let's go!"

Suzie frowned, she grabbed Malky's arm. "Wait a minute, Malky. You KNOW that they did it?" Had she been completely wrong all along?

His whole manner was suddenly confident and smug as he turned to answer her. "It was her cousins. Jenna saw them there outside the flats on the night of the fire, when they were supposed to be at the family party."

Perhaps it was the cousins, but Suzie struggled to be convinced, something just didn't fit. Was it all too easy and neat? She teased it around in her head for a moment or two.

OMG! She had just remembered something she had heard the other day. "Malky! If the cousins set the flats on fire, what if they come after Jenna? What exactly did Jenna say about her cousins?"

"She always said they were pretty scary and kept telling me not to cross them, so, yeah, they are not to be messed with. Why?"

Suzie bit her lip, she had to say something but even thinking about it sounded over dramatic. Nonetheless, she had to tell them.

"I heard something the other day, I think it was on the TV, about these 'honour killings'. They said that a girl had been killed by her own family because she wouldn't marry the man that had been picked out for her, and she had been going about in modern clothes and seeing boys and things like that. They said she was a shame on the family so they abducted her and later the police found out that she'd been killed by her own family!"

It seemed even more horrific and real, now that she had said it out loud. "You don't think they would do that to Jenna, do you? We've got to get her away before they find her."

*****

Danger. It was everywhere.

Jenna could feel it all along her skin and in her bones; every nerve strung out and jangling. Just when you thought everything was going fine, that was when it all went wrong.

She knocked at the door of the house, but there was no answer. She'd felt a bit silly knocking; she knew no one lived here any more, but it seemed the right thing to do, less scary somehow. The door swung open when she pushed it, revealing a narrow hallway with peeling sheets of wallpaper bent over like wide leaves reaching out from the wall. She had to lean to the side to avoid touching them as she made for the door at the far end.

It was exactly as Malky had described it, so she knew she was in the right place, but that didn't make it any less creepy. She hated dirty, dark places but she knew she had to do this.

Pushing open the door she looked around. The only window, a mess of broken glass and twisted metal spars, let in some light but the majority of the room was in darkness.

She stepped further into the room and screamed softly as she felt a mass of stickiness coat her face and hair. She shuddered, fighting to wipe away the clinging spider webs.

They stuck to her fingers, her eyes, her lips, her hair. She hated the idea of anything getting stuck in her hair and now she felt like her whole body was crawling with spiders.

It was a few minutes before she could think coherently again and even then she could hardly stop shuddering. Tears collected unbidden at the corner of her eyes but she knew she had to pull herself together.

Where was Malky? Would he come? He had to. He'd promised. She knew it would be all right when he arrived. The worst thing was being alone.

What if something had happened and he couldn't get away? What if he changed his mind? She forced herself to stop thinking like that. It only made things worse.

Worse? A shrill, wobbly laugh spilled from her lips but she clamped down hard on it. It could hardly be any worse, could it?

Why couldn't they leave her alone. It was her life, she never meant anyone any harm. She never wanted much, just to be loved, to be free to make her own decisions. She wished she was still the little girl her father would swing up into the air and call his little princess. She had known then that he loved her. She longed to go back to those times when she was a child, when things were simple, but that wasn't possible.

What if Malky didn't come?

She stood in the same spot for ages, not wanting to move in case she stepped into another web or stood on any of the debris that littered the floor. All around her were the dirty sharp bits of the couch that had a tangle of metal springs erupting from the centre. The floor was littered with pieces of broken glass and piles of empty boxes full of rubbish. She just hoped there were no rats. She knew that if anything started rustling on the floor she would run. Cousins or not, she would run.

How long should she wait? They were expecting her home soon and when she didn't appear her parents would tell her aunt that she was missing and then she wouldn't be safe anywhere.

But she knew Malky was right, they would never look for her in a place like this. She hoped he would come and get her soon, they needed to get away as quickly as they could.

A car drove by. It slowed down and stopped.

She held her breath, trying not to move; trying to listen with every part of her body to what was happening outside. She could hardly hear anything except the thundering of her heartbeat and a sound like crashing sea in her ears.

A moment later the car drove off again. Was there someone there, had they got out of the car? Was that footsteps she could hear outside?

She shivered and stuffed her fist in her mouth to stop a sound escaping.

The front door swung open and a tall shadow blocked the light from outside. Jenna tried not to scream but a soft cry escaped unbidden. "Malky?"

The figure took a few steps down the hallway.

"Hello, Jenna!" Hasan's voice filled the space between them. She could hear his self-satisfied smile even if she couldn't see it.

CHAPTER 31

Malky had tried to call Jenna a couple of times on her mobile but there had been no reply, it had gone to messages immediately. He was feeling very twitchy by the time they withdrew money from the cash machine. Even running part of the way it still took them a good 15 minutes to get to the house.

Jenna was still not answering her phone and Malky had all sorts of terrible images in his head, which didn't help at all. What Suzie had told them had terrified him. Before that he hadn't really believed that her cousins would actually harm her, but now he kept picturing her being dragged from the house by Hasan and his brother, and bundled into a car, never to be seen again.

"We've got to be quiet, we've got the element of surprise," Malky said in a loud stage whisper, holding his arm in front of Jack and Suzie so that he prevented them from running right up to the front door. "I'll go first."

Jack shook his head and rolled his eyes at Malky's melodramatic tone, but let him go in first anyway.

The front door creaked open and he could see the door was open through into the room beyond the hallway. Malky stepped forward slowly, walking carefully, as if the floors were about to give way, and flattening himself against the wall so that no one could see him from the room beyond. He motioned to Jack and Suzie to do the same. His heart was thundering, terrified, but he couldn't help feeling a bit excited. He was like 007 about to confront his nemesis and he kept reminding himself that James Bond wouldn't be scared.

He heard something from inside the room — a soft footstep. And before he could move a tall figure appeared.

Malky almost swallowed his tongue. His feet were cemented to the floor and his breath had stopped. He could understand what folk meant when they said people's faces drained of all colour. He felt as if all the blood in his body had suddenly poured into his boots, leaving him reeling in shock.

"You must be Malky." Hasan loomed huge in the doorway. "And you've brought your friends, too, have you? Well, you'd all better come in then. Jenna was waiting for you, but I got here just in time, I think."

It was more of a command than an invitation. Malky forced his feet forward, unable to drag his eyes from Jenna's cousin's dark, forbidding face.

Jack and Suzie followed Malky and there was Jenna standing in the middle of the room. Suzie searched for signs of mistreatment but she seemed to be fine aside from the black streaks around her eyes where her tears had ruined her normally perfectly make-up.

Jenna's eyes flickered from Malky to her cousin and back again and she started to cry softly, biting her lip.

"Jenna, are you okay?" Suzie asked with a glance back at Hasan, who was standing between them and the door.

Jenna sniffed and nodded her head.

"How did you find her?" demanded Malky.

"It wasn't difficult. Jenna is fine, now." Hasan's voice was loud and harsh, echoing around the room. "She's just had a change of heart."

Suzie turned to him. He towered over her but she was now so angry that she didn't care. She hated being told what to do and it made her furious that this man should be able to push Jenna around with his threats.

"Just because you forced her to! You have no right to do this," she barked up at him. "You can't make her do what you want. We won't let you."

Out of the corner of her eye she saw Malky and Jack nodding in agreement. She felt the encouraging comfort of Jack's hand in hers, but a moment later she was caught and mesmerised when Hasan turned his hard, dark eyes on her. Suzie wondered for a moment if someone could actually make your heart stop beating, just by looking at you. He looked as if he could do just that.

"Suzie, no." Jenna's voice was a soft plea. "It's okay, Suzie, really."

Hearing the normally confident Jenna sound so pathetic only made her even more furious and her anger gave her courage. "No, it's not okay, Jenna. He shouldn't be able to make you do anything he wants just because he threatens you. It's a free country, and we won't let him get away with it."

"Is that right?" Hasan's voice had a dangerous kind of humorous edge to it. He was laughing at her.

"Yes, it is," Malky said, coming to stand beside Suzie. "And there's four of us and just one of you."

A car drew up outside. A door slammed and they could all hear footsteps approaching the house. Suzie realised that Hasan was about to get reinforcements. If she was going to do anything it had to be now.

"I've heard all about these 'honour killings' and we won't let you take Jenna away so that you can kill her. See..." Suzie pulled her phone out of her pocket and showed him that she had already dialled a number. "I'm calling the police and all I need to do now is press this and they will come." Suzie hoped that she was right. What if it was just some switchboard that took ages to explain what help they needed?

The footsteps outside had almost reached the door.

There was a deep silence in the room. It was as if the world had stopped spinning for just a moment and they were all frozen in time. Suzie watched Hasan, searching every inch of his face, every tiny muscle movement, to see if she could predict how he would react. He stared, his eyes boring into her, scarily unreadable.

Hasan suddenly opened his mouth and started to laugh.

Suzie stared at him, terrified of this almost more than the scowl he had worn earlier. She looked round at Jack and Malky but they were as confused as she was. He suddenly stopped laughing and started shaking his head at her, the amusement turning to a more sinister anger. He curled his lip and sneered at her. "You...stupid...little...girl!"

A cry came from behind her. It was Jenna. "Dad!"

Her father stood framed in the doorway, his arms held wide for her. Jenna rushed into his embrace.

The atmosphere in the room changed.

Confused, Suzie looked from Jenna to her father and her cousin. "I don't understand," she mumbled.

Hasan scowled at her. "Of course you don't. Did you seriously think we would hurt Jenna?" He shook his head. "She's my cousin. I've known her since she was a baby. I look out for her and the family. We just wanted to stop her doing something stupid."

"But I thought.... Jenna?"

Jenna pulled herself out of her father's arms. "Thank you, Suzie. I never thought you would stand up for me like that. But Hasan is not trying to harm me. He would never do that. My family are not like that, they love me."

Suzie had never heard Malky sound so upset as when he spoke now. "But you said you were frightened of him? You said you wanted to run away, with me."

"I'm sorry, Malky, I realised that I couldn't do it in the end.

Hasan came to find me and to tell me how upset my parents were when they discovered I had taken my things and wasn't planning to come back home. I didn't realise how bad I would feel about leaving them." She turned to her father and gently hugged him. Her father smiled down at her.

Jenna moved towards Malky. "I hope you will understand? I'm sorry, Malky, but I can't go away with you, not if it means choosing between you and my family." He scowled at her betrayal and shrugged her off.

*****

Malky's phone started to ring as Jenna and her cousin drove off in her father's car.

"Yeah, What?"

Suzie and Jack could hear Malky's mother's high-pitched voice almost shouting down the phone at him.

"Yeah, I know. I'll be there, Mum." He made a face and held the phone away from his ear while she ranted some more at him. "I know I'm late but... I just said so! I'll be there!" He turned off his phone and thrust it into his jacket pocket. "I'd better go, she's at the police station and I was supposed to be there half an hour ago."

"Hey, Malky!" Jack caught up with him, just before he crossed the road. "What about that cash I gave you?"

Malky grabbed it from his back pocket and handed it over. "Here."

He walked away from Jack and Suzie and crossed the road, automatically heading towards the centre of town. He couldn't believe what had just happened. Jenna had discarded him as if he was nobody, as if he didn't matter. He kicked at an old can lying on the pavement and looked for something else to kick, or break or thump. He shouldered his way past an old man on the street and ignored the angry complaints.

Why had she done that? One moment she wanted him to up and leave town with her, and the next she was all pals again with her dad and her cousin. What the heck was she playing at?

He was crossing the park when he caught sight of the apartment block, still blackened with smoke, all the windows blown out. There was no way he was going to take the rap for this, no way she was getting off with it, with throwing him to the dogs. After all he had done for her this was how she repaid him.

He had just wanted to protect her, but she didn't care, she was just going to ignore him and pretend he didn't matter. After all he had done for her. He did matter and he would show her. He would show them all.

CHAPTER 32

Malky headed to the front door of the flats where Jenna lived. He pulled his hood up to hide his face. He was on a mission, like a secret agent or a detective in one of his favourite TV shows. He felt important, he had things to do and he had to make sure no one saw him doing them.

Glancing behind him he scanned the area outside the flats. Suzie and Jack had been out front in the park, but they had gone now. He checked to make sure there wasn't anyone else hanging around before he ran in and up the stairs to the first turn in the stairwell.

He stopped again, wielding an imaginary pistol in two hands, holding it in the air, pointing to the ceiling. He leaned back against the wall as he peered down towards the entrance, as all the best cops did, to make sure no one was coming in behind him. His heart was thumping — whether with fear or excitement he didn't know or care.

He was determined to stop Jenna's father seeing the photos Suzie had taken. He'd seen Suzie coming out of the flats so he knew she had put them through the letterbox. He knew she would do it, just like she'd threatened.

So now he had no choice. He had to destroy them before Jenna's father came home or her cousins would come after him. He didn't need Jenna's warning, he knew they were bad news. He didn't like to admit how scared he was of them, they were well known locally and what he had heard about them had terrified him.

After Suzie had revealed her intentions, he'd made up his mind and gone off to get the things he'd need. Jenna had said everyone would be at the party, so he knew there was no one at home. By the time they all got back the photos would be history.

It was all he could think about and if it meant that her dad's house got a bit damaged in the fire, well, what did he care. Her dad hated him, so it would be a lesson. And no one would know it was him, Malky, because all the evidence would be destroyed in the fire.

He pulled the rags and matches out of his pocket. It almost didn't work at first, the matches kept on fizzling out. But then it did. Job done!

Malky was already running out of the building by the time tiny tendrils of smoke curled and danced through the letterbox. His footsteps beat a staccato on the pavement, disappearing out into the night.

*****

The smoke gathered behind the door. Small wisps escaping into the passageway were an indication of the choking black clouds that now inhabited the flat.

The woman barely noticed at first, her mind on other things, but insidiously the smoke spiralled into the air, tainting it with a familiar smell that triggered painful memories. In the dim light from the streetlamps, the open doorway was becoming hazy, filling up with smoke. Not her cigarette smoke, there was too much for that. Real smoke, like something on fire.

She froze, gripping the banister tightly with her one free hand and letting her cigarette end drop from between her fingers. A moment later she was running, through the hazy smoke and out into the night.

Her cigarette end tumbled slowly through the air.

End over end, its smouldering tip was a bright glowing spark in the darkness as it spun in a lazy spiral, tumbling and spinning down into the shadows.

In the basement it landed softly, nestling in a bed of tinder-dry rubbish. Warmed by the glowing tip, the edge of a cloth started to turn brown as the paper lying beside it became singed. The words on the leaflet — "Fire Safety — what to do in case of.... ' — were the first to disappear in a tiny lick of flame.

CHAPTER 33

Jack took Suzie's hand. "That was great, what you did just now, standing up to her cousin when you thought he was going to hurt Jenna."

She blushed. "It was probably pretty stupid. I've never been so scared in my life, but I was so angry I just didn't stop to think. What if her cousin had been as dangerous as we thought he was? We could all have been in real trouble."

Jack grinned at her. "Naw, he'd never have got past all of us!"

"I hope Malky's okay. He seemed really crushed when Jenna went home with her dad."

"Yeah, but I think he'll bounce back. He always does. You know Malky. Look, I've got to go back home soon. Mum said I could only come out if I promised to be back by 7pm. The police want me back in to see them first thing in the morning. You want to go to Joe's for a coffee or something?"

Suzie could see how worried he was and she felt a bit bad that she'd not thought about that at all. It had to be weighing on his mind. But with all that had happened with Jenna there hadn't been much time to speak to Jack on her own.

"Sounds good to me."

*****

When they got to Joe's she ordered a latte and sat playing with the froth.

"Jack, I've been thinking, about who started the fire in the flats the other night."

"What about it?"

She stirred the froth into a pile in the centre of the cup,

watching it spin. "If Hasan and his brother wouldn't do anything to harm the family, why would they have started the fire?"

"Perhaps they knew no one was home. None of Jenna's family were there, they were all at the party."

"Yes, I know, but still..." She stirred the cup again, faster, destroying her carefully constructed foam mountain.

"You think it was someone else? Who?"

Suzie scooped up a spoonful of milky foam and tasted it as she hesitated, not sure how to say what she was thinking. "I really don't know if I should even say this, but you know those photos I put through their letterbox."

Jack frowned at her. "Yes, what about them?"

"I told Malky I was going to do it."

She watched Jack consider what she had said and saw the understanding slowly change his expression.

"You think Malky...? No! I know he does some stupid things but that is beyond even him, isn't it?"

She raised her eyebrows and shrugged, lifting her cup to take a gulp of hot coffee. She never took her eyes off Jack, automatically wiping the line of froth from her top lip as she watched to see how he would react.

"You really think it was him?"

Suzie could see him starting to think about Malky, considering whether it could be true. She looked at Jack and nodded, a little reluctantly. "The more I think about it, the way he's been behaving recently..."

Jack got up, almost knocking over his chair. He grabbed Suzie's jacket and handed it to her. "C'mon. We'd better find him. In the mood he's in I don't think he's about to go to the police."

"What do you mean?"

"We've got to stop him, before he does something really stupid."

"You know where he's gone, don't you." Suzie scrambled after him between the chairs and out into the Mall.

Jack nodded. "I've a pretty good idea, but we'd better hurry."

They ran down the High Street. Jack led Suzie towards a small shop close to where Malky lived. As they approached it they saw him stuffing something into the pocket of his jeans as he closed the door,.

"Hey, Malky!" Jack shouted, waving to him.

At first Malky looked as if he was going to pretend he hadn't heard Jack. But then he looked up and stood watching them cross the street.

"What you doing?" Jack asked, staring at Malky's bulging pocket. "What's you got?"

Malky glared at him. "Nothing. None of your business anyway."

"Malky." Suzie tried to smile at him but she was finding it hard. "We're your friends."

"Yeah, right!"

"We know what you did." Jack stood right in front of him so there was nowhere for him to run.

"You know nothing, either of you."

Suzie glared at him. "We know you started the fire in the flats."

"You can't prove it. You can't prove anything!" he snarled at her.

Jack held out his hand. "Let's see what you just bought, then."

"Go mind your own business."

Jack pushed him against the wall and held him there.

Malky was stocky but Jack was taller and used to being the one in control.

"Leave me alone, Jack. You're no saint, yourself."

"Never said I was." Jack grabbed the can of lighter fuel out of Malky's pocket. "It's not clever, Malky. Someone almost died in that fire. I don't think you meant that to happen, but if you do it again it might be different this time."

"You need to forget Jenna, Malky," Suzie said. "It's not worth getting yourself into more trouble."

"All right for you to say."

Malky's phone went off and he tried to ignore it.

"Aren't you going to answer it?" Suzie asked.

Malky took it out of his pocket and looked at it. "It's just my mum." He turned his phone off.

"If you don't go they'll work out it was you, and come looking for you. Then you'll be in worse trouble."

"No they won't, Jack." Malky shook his head. "Anyway, they'll have to catch me first." He pushed Jack away from him and took off down the street. Suzie started to follow, shouting after him to stop, but Jack called her back.

"But shouldn't we go after him, Jack?"

"There's no point, Suzie. Let him go."

CHAPTER 34

The following afternoon Suzie got a call from Jack and they arranged to meet at Joe's. When she got there he was already sitting at one of the tables. with a.

"Hi Suzie. I got you this." He nodded at the frothy latte in front of him. "That ok?"

"Yes, that's great, thanks. How did you get on? I've been worrying about you all morning."

"I'm okay. Nothing has been decided yet but with good conduct and no record they say I'll probably get off with probation and some community service. But they want me and mum to get some counselling. Probably be a load of rubbish!"

"Yeah, probably." Suzie laughed. "What about Malky, have you heard from him?"

"The police told me today that they caught him at the railway station last night and he's being questioned about the fire. They pretty much know it was him, but it's worse than that because that woman, the baby's mother...she died last night."

"Oh no!"

"So now Malky's likely to be charged with manslaughter as well as firesetting."

Suzie was silent for a moment, it was hard to take it all in. She'd had her suspicions but it was altogether different to know for certain that it had been Malky, and worse that the woman had died because of his actions.

"It's all my fault. I caused it." She bit her lip and stared out the window, not wanting to look at Jack. "If I'd not told Malky what I was going to do with the photos..."

"No, I don't think you can blame yourself, Suzie. You didn't start the fire, Malky did, and you saw him yesterday, he was ready to do it again. You can't blame yourself for that. We all make mistakes and we all do stupid things. And sometimes people get hurt when we don't mean them to." He hesitated for a moment. "I should know!"

Suzie sipped her coffee. "How is your Gran?"

"She's a bit better. She should get out of the hospital in a few days."

"That's great, Jack."

"My mother's still fuming at me, though!"

"I can imagine!" Suzie smiled and raised her mug to her mouth. But before she drank from it she said, "Jack, how did the Police know it was definitely Malky? Did he admit it?"

"I think so. They said they had suspected it was him and found some evidence on his clothes; lighter fuel, like the stuff he was buying yesterday. They said he used it to start the fire. I still find it hard to believe he was actually going to start another fire. What was he thinking?"

Suzie shook her head. "Probably a knee-jerk reaction. He's always been a bit like that. He never thinks things through and he was really angry after what happened with Jenna, but it was just plain stupid."

Jack's phone buzzed. He picked it up and read the message. "It's my mum. She says Gran's getting out of hospital tomorrow morning!"

"That's great."

"I meant to tell you, I got a call from Jenna last night. She was shocked because the police had just told her father that it was Malky who started the fire in their flat. She wanted to know if I knew. She said she'd had a long talk with her parents and they had promised not to force her to marry that guy Pavan."

"At least that's something."

"That's not all. Turns out his family had threatened to destroy her aunt's business if the wedding didn't go through. Her aunt had been really worried and that was what they had all been arguing about when Jenna overheard them. It was when they realised she had run away that her father told the police the whole story. The police are going to investigate it."

"Good."

"You just couldn't make it up, could you?" Jack and shook his head. "So, Suzie, what you doing tonight? Want to go and see a film?"

Suzie thought for a moment. "Okay, as long as it's pure escapism and not anything that reminds me of the last few days!"

"So not Towering Inferno, then?"

"Definitely not!" Suzie scowled.

Jack finished his coffee. "Okay then, let's see what's on."

"Sounds good to me."

Spider

Linda Strachan

ISBN: 978-1-905537-068 RRP: £6.99, paperback. Also available as an ebook

SPIDER

'Fast-paced and uncompromising' — *The Herald*

'A gritty, realistic story with conflicted characters that get under your skin and prick your conscience.' — *Waterstone's*

'Linda Strachan is such a compelling writer.' — *Armadillo*

A hard-hitting and provocative novel about teenage love, loyalty and fast cars. Spider is on his last warning. If he's caught joyriding again he'll be sent down, no questions asked. He's trying to stick to the straight and narrow but his girlfriend Deanna and mate Andy reckon he should risk one last run. Spider is an adrenaline-fuelled ride — a compelling glimpse into a life spinning out of control.

'A triumph of teenage fiction. The author skilfully juggles the voices of three very different teenagers — Spider, Andy and Deanna — in a pacy, touching story that never palls. A compelling, insightful intertwining of credible characters.' —
The Irish Examiner

'It's an intense ride. You can almost hear the wheels spin, smell the tyres burn. Spider believes it's entirely his fault for drawing others into his web. Strachan, however, allows the reader to see a bigger picture of leaders and their followers.'
— *The Scotsman*

ISBN: 978-1-905537-204 RRP: £6.99, paperback. Also available as an ebook

DEAD BOY TALKING

Josh has 25 minutes left to live.

Lying alone in a pool of blood, Josh hasn't much time to think. Yesterday he stabbed his best mate, and now it's happened to him. But there are questions he can't get out of his head. Like, how did he get into this mess? Will anyone find him in time? Will his girlfriend forgive him, and what really happened to his older brother?

As his life slips away, the events of the last 24 hours start to look very different...

"I was totally hooked from the very first sentence"

My Favourite Books

"The fast pace and direct approach will have a particular appeal to reluctant readers. A definite must have for any school library."

The Bookette